Jerusalem Rising: Adah's Journey

Barbara M. Britton

Jerusalem Rising: Adah's Journey
COPYRIGHT 2017 by Barbara M. Britton

Contact Information: titleadmin@pelicanbookgroup.com

Cover Art by *Nicola Martinez*

Harbourlight Books, a division of Pelican Ventures, LLC
www.pelicanbookgroup.com PO Box 1738 *Aztec, NM * 87410

Harbourlight Books sail and mast logo is a trademark of Pelican Ventures, LLC

Publishing History
First Harbourlight Edition, 2017
Electronic Edition ISBN 978-1-61116-938-6
Paperback Edition ISBN 978-1-61116-940-9
Published in the United States of America

Dedication

To my parents, who love me and encourage me. I am blessed to have such wonderful role models.

Acknowledgements

This book would not have been possible without the help of so many people. My family has been my cheering section throughout my publishing journey. I am blessed to have their love and encouragement.

A big thank you goes to my editor, Megan Lee, who corrects my mistakes, and champions my stories, and to Nicola Martinez for her continuing support of my writing and for her wise Christian leadership at Pelican.

My marvelous critique partner, Betsy Norman, was at it again. She makes me a better writer and she is a wonderful friend. The Barnes & Noble Brainstormers keep me focused on my stories and are a highlight of my week. Thank you, Jill Bevers, Liz Czukas, Sandy Goldsworthy, Karen Miller, Betsy Norman, Liz Steiner, Sandee Turriff, and Christine Welman.

My Mo's Crew friends encourage me along this writing journey. Thank you, Justen Hisle, Mary Hughes, Leigh Morgan and Edie Ramer.

I have a huge support system within the WisRWA community. Thank you, Carla Cullen, Brenda Nelson-Davis, Tricia Quinnies, and Maureen Welli. Likewise, I am grateful for my friends in my SCBWI community, and the ACFW community. My church family in Wisconsin and countrywide has been a huge blessing to me as always.

And last, but definitely not least, to the Lord God Almighty, for giving me the gift of creativity and breath each day to write these stories. I am a cancer survivor, and not a day goes by that I don't praise the Lord for his healing. To God be the glory.

Also Available

Providence: Hannah's Journey
Building Benjamin: Naomi's Journey

1

*How deserted lies the city, once so full of people! How like a
widow is she, who once was great among the nations!*
Lamentations 1:1

Seventeen-year-old Adah *bat* Shallum breathed
deep. Deep enough to carry the pomegranate, cassia,
and aloe scents from the length of her nose to the
depths of her lungs. Was this fragrance a treasure or a
stench? She trusted her senses. Her patience had
produced a precious perfume worth several silver
coins. Possibly some gold ones too. Careful not to spill
a single drop, she poured her afternoon's labor into
small glazed jars, and lined them one finger length
from the edge of the shelf and one thumb width apart.
A piece of whittled poplar closed every opening and
kept her fragrance captive.

"Adah. Judith." The summons echoed down the
street. A harsh inflection deepened her father's voice.

She peeked through a hole in the wall—a rough-
edged reminder of Nebuchadnezzar's siege—and
spied her father's forward-leaning march. Wiping her
hands on a clean rag, she scurried around the acacia
wood table, a centerpiece to the small space she
recently called her own. She crossed the threshold of
her storeroom and hastened into the dirt lane.

Judith stood across the street in the doorway to

their home, forehead furrowed, hands clasped. Did her sister think the booming call was Adah's fault?

She fingered the beads of her necklace. Her months of worries had worn the sandalwood orbs slick as sapphires.

"Girls," her father huffed, scarlet-faced. "Dress your mother. The governor is on the outskirts of the city with an escort of cavalry. We must be ready to receive him."

How could this be? Her father had not mentioned a visit, and he ruled a half-district of Jerusalem. "Did the governor not send word of his arrival?"

Her father shook his turban-wrapped head. "Make haste. I must set up a banquet." He kissed her forehead and stumbled as he approached Judith.

Adah reached out to steady him. "Stay a moment and have something to drink. Preparations can wait."

Judith rushed to aid their father. "A few sips of water and you will be ready to return."

Dashing into the cooking courtyard, Adah located a pitcher and poured water into a cup. Her father was too old to be racing across the city in such heat. A servant or neighbor could have relayed the message. But then she would not have seen the importance her father placed on the governor's visit.

She found her father in the shade of the overhang and offered him the cup. He drank as if a fire raged in his throat.

"*Shalom*, my daughters." With a deep breath and a reluctant sigh, her father gathered his robe and trudged in the direction of the temple. "Do not be idle."

What happened to the governor's messenger? A nobleman did not travel without preparations being made for his arrival. And if her father had no knowledge of the governor's journey then he had no time to prepare an offering. Let no one say the household of Shallum was inhospitable.

Adah grasped her sister's arm. "You must tend to Mother. I have an errand in the marketplace."

"Where are you running off to now? You have been absent all day." Judith scowled. "Bread does not bake itself."

Adah wiggled her oil-infused fingers close to her sister's face. "If I had helped cook with these scents in my skin, the food would have been spoiled." *And I would have no gift to uphold our family's honor.*

Judith stilled Adah's wave and sniffed the fragrance wafting from her hand. "This is new. Pour me a small jar of your perfume and all is forgiven."

"As you wish." Adah backed across the street toward her storeroom. "And do not forget mother's embroidered sash. It was a gift from the governor."

Judith rolled her shoulders as if an insult had escaped her sister's lips. "Mother will not know one adornment from another."

"Oh, yes she will. The weaves are stored up here." Adah tapped her temple. "And arrange a robe for me. *Toda raba*, sister."

Adah hurried up the straightest street in Jerusalem toward the temple. She passed the rubble of homes abandoned by her people. Waist-high walls and roofless dwellings marred the landscape of the City of David.

Running at a messenger's pace, she raced through a maze of streets and alleys before arriving at a small marketplace. Booths, nestled near the Horse Gate, served the priests and visitors who had coins to buy artisan wares. Zipporah's corner station stood empty. Where was the bartering woman? Why would a merchant be absent before afternoon prayer?

She sprinted down the hill by the battered city wall to Zipporah's home and knocked on the door with an irreverent fervor. Later she would ask to be forgiven for her rudeness.

No answer came forth. Adah slumped against the worn lumber, huffing like a slave girl. Sweat pooled beneath her head covering.

"My mother is not home. She has gone to the well," said a familiar male voice.

Praise God. She scrambled to her feet. "Othniel, you are a vision. Hurry and help me. I have coins today."

Othniel slung his satchel near the door. The little storm of unsettled dust rising from the ground almost matched the amount clinging to his dark, curly hair. "What kind of greeting is this?"

"A hasty one." Adah shook the folds of her skirt to loosen any dirt. "Our governor is coming to Jerusalem and my father is not prepared for his arrival."

"Doesn't Nehemiah send letters?" Othniel scratched his stubbled chin. He seemed in as much of a hurry as a bloated mule.

"None that my father saw," she said.

His eyebrows raised as understanding brightened his eyes. "But someone received them?"

And she knew who. A nobleman never traveled unannounced. Her father ruled a half-district of Jerusalem, but Rephaiah also ruled a half-district, and no one caught him or his brood of sons off guard.

"Come now." Her pulse sped as if in a race. "Open the room where your mother keeps her wares and help me find a polished pearl jar. I've seen it in the marketplace." She urged him down the alley next to his home, wishing she could give him a powerful push. "My family has need of it."

"I should warn you. I have labored in the grove." His steps still lumbered. "I smell like a dung heap."

"My nose has been in oils all afternoon. To me, you have the aroma of a blossom." She smiled big.

"Good. For the storeroom is small and I believe the gift you seek is in a cedar box on the top shelf." Othniel opened the door to a storage area near the back of his family's dwelling. As she entered, he inhaled. "Ah, is that a lily note? I do not know whether I should sleep or till the soil."

"Cassia and fruit." She sniffed her fingertips. "Though I have been stroking sandalwood." She lifted the chrysolite and wooden beads around her neck.

"That is what my trees look like. All brown. If only I had olives as green as your gems." He laughed short and loud, but desperation strangled his normally lighthearted tone.

Her smile vanished as he turned toward the shelves of trinkets. The once-full room held only a few tapestries, beaded veils, and decorated pottery, items easily disregarded when a family needed to eat.

While Othniel searched for the crate that held her jar, she stuffed loose strands of hair under her head covering. With her sprint through the market, she probably resembled a ruffled bird.

He held up the emblazoned wooden case as if it were a king's scepter. "This is what you have need of?" He opened the carved cedar box and revealed the tiny pearl bottle with the gold stopper.

She practically leapt into the air and grabbed the prize. Producing three silver coins from her pouch, she said, "I am in your debt."

He did not reach for her payment. "No. I am in yours. For my mother asks less than this sum."

"This item is worth every coin. Please, take them." She pushed the silver into his palm.

As his fingers closed, his calluses weighed heavy upon her skin.

If only Othniel's family could keep her payment, but she knew these same pieces of silver would come back to the city officials for a land tax. She turned to leave and remembered her upbringing. "How is your family? Does your vineyard fare any better than the grove?"

"We have already discussed a dung heap." He started to grin but his smile faltered. "Without water the vines wither. And without money, my father withers. All will be lost if it does not rain soon."

"Then I will pray for our God to open a rain cloud above your lands." Truly she would, for she knew Othniel and his brothers worked harder than most, but the drought did not reward their labor or increase their family's income.

"I hope *Adonai* listens to you. Now go and fill that jar." He closed the door behind them. "If it is with the scent you are wearing then it will be a priceless gift."

Her cheeks warmed from his praise of her perfume. Othniel was one of the few who supported her trade. When he found a flower in the fields it appeared on the table in her storeroom.

She back-stepped quickly down the alley. "Tell your mother I am grateful."

He held up the coins and nodded. "This payment eases the worries of a fifth son. Perhaps you are my vision today."

"*Shalom*, my friend." She would be no one's vision if she did not hurry home, remove her oil-stained clothes, and be dressed in time for the banquet.

She ran down the straight street through the middle of the city. Why couldn't there be a breeze this afternoon?

After arriving home, she donned a striped malachite robe, while her mother waited in the front quarter of their home. When all the ladies of the house were dressed, Adah and Judith took their customary positions on each side of their mother. Adah stood on the left and Judith stood on the right. Each daughter supported the wife of Shallum as they made the journey to the officials' chamber. Guiding her mother came naturally now. Rocks, juts in the street, and wayward goats were warned about without a thought.

"I wish we were not rushed this day," Adah said as they neared the columned meeting place adjacent to the temple. She briefly let go of her mother and stuffed a stubborn ringlet under her head covering. Her other hand clutched the cedar perfume box. "Two priests are at the entrance. Straight ahead of Judith."

Her mother nodded to the priests, and after a few strides she said, "Let us uphold your father's name and see that the governor does not forget our household."

"Like he forgot to announce his visit?" Judith's voice rumbled with contempt.

Adah and Judith exchanged a raised-eyebrow look.

Inside the meeting room, finely robed magistrates, noblemen, and ephod-laden priests milled around the governor as if he were the cow and they his freshly birthed calves. Even though her father had left early, Rephaiah, the other ruler, had already stationed himself at the governor's right hand.

The procession of greeters filled the center aisle of the main room. Rephaiah's sons, all eight of them, hovered in back of Adah, Judith, and her mother. Their breath on the back of her neck felt like a storm wind.

A waft of spit-cooked meat caused her stomach to rumble.

Judith glared at her. Who could hear such a small belly gurgle with all the clamoring of the people?

"Five paces and we will stand in front of Nehemiah." Adah glanced at the mosaic on the wall and smiled as if her conversation were polite banter.

"How low does my sash hang?" her mother asked. "I do not want my knee to catch when I bow."

Adah eyed her mother's robe. "The beading ends below your hip. You will not fall at the governor's feet."

"Do you not trust my abilities?" Judith took a step and eased their mother forward.

"Of course I do, dear." Mother patted Judith's hand. "But I have not seen the governor for a while and not since —"

"My wife, Elisheba." Her father's arm swung wide.

Her mother bobbed. "And my twin daughters, Judith and Adah." She hung back and let Judith give her greeting to the governor. After all, she was the oldest daughter if only by a few screams.

Nehemiah stood shoulder-to-shoulder with her father, not towering, but with a stature to command authority. He was not old, but somehow his face held grooves far deeper than his years. A golden fringe hemmed the governor's sleeves making his every move grand.

"Adah." Her name flew from her father's lips as though she had done something wrong.

Had she been staring? A snicker from behind stiffened her posture.

"Governor." She bent low. "My father speaks of how you have found King Artaxerxes' favor and that of his queen. The king will receive our taxes, but I hope you will see that Queen Damaspia receives this perfume as a gift from Jerusalem." She opened the tiny cedar chest and displayed the pearl vessel. "The fragrant oils were gathered not far from our wall."

Nehemiah reached to take the box. "This is truly a gift from my city. Bless you, daughter of Shallum. May the Queen remember us fondly." Holding the gift to his chest, the governor whispered a prayer. When he finished, tears glistened in his eyes. "I will send a messenger to the Queen at once. May the City of David be a delight to her as it is to all of us."

Toda raba, Othniel. If only he knew what his timely arrival meant to her.

Her father ushered his small family to the side of the procession so Rephaiah's sons could be paraded before the governor.

"That was the errand you had this afternoon." Judith's face glowed like a freshly oiled lamp. It seemed any insult she thought Adah had cast by leaving in a rush was long forgotten. "You could have mentioned it."

"I did not know if I would be successful, but your jar is by your bed."

Her mother sighed. "Someone describe the gift to me. I do not want to guess all night."

Adah released her steadying hold. "Take mother to sit with the women and describe the vessel. I will serve us some drinks."

Leaving the spacious hall, Adah headed toward a courtyard set up for the women. In a nearby tent, servants filled cups with water and wine for the coming meal. Before she reached the opened tent flaps, a cool shiver bathed her skin.

"Daughter of Shallum," a man bellowed.

She turned to find Gershom *ben* Rephaiah, the ruler's son, closing in on her ground. His lips were but a thin line and his eyes were those of a mourner, not a rejoicer.

Had his father finished the introductions of his eight sons already?

Gershom crossed his arms, displaying his gold rings. "Gifts are to be given by the officials upon arrival. Does the king's household not have enough oils?"

Where was Gershom's proper greeting? Flattery usually preceded a rebuke. She smiled at the ruler's son, but inwardly she scolded his insult.

"You saw the perfume, then? My father had other business to attend to since the notice of the governor's arrival was late." She emphasized the tardiness of the announcement, even though Gershom, his father, and his brothers had not seemed flustered by Nehemiah's visit.

"Do not fool yourself, girl." Gershom kept a respectable distance but his voice assaulted her ears. "Whatever business Nehemiah has with Jerusalem will be dealt with by the men of this city. You have no standing here."

Her cheeks flamed. What did Gershom care if she bestowed a present on Nehemiah? Except, perhaps, that he and his brothers had brought nothing of importance. This night would not be ruined by this fool.

"Whatever business? You mean you do not know the governor's decrees? Perhaps you should be talking to him and not to me." She turned, waved off a servant girl, and collected three cups from a table. Her chin rose slightly as she sauntered by Gershom.

Gershom blocked her escape. "We do not have to be adversaries. Our fathers rule together."

She stepped away from him. "Apparently not at all times."

Shaking his head, he leaned in. "What a shame your father finally had children in his old age only to be cursed with two girls. I will pray he lives a long life."

Adah met his dismissive gaze and held it until he rocked back on his heels. "See to your father's dealings and leave me to my own." She cocked her head toward the door to the officials' hall. "I do believe the men are dining inside."

Gershom stomped off and almost collided with Judith as she rounded the courtyard wall.

Judith muttered an apology and let Gershom pass. "What did you say to anger him?"

"I believe it's something I did." Adah handed a cup to her sister.

Judith's eyes grew wide. "You found out the governor's business?"

"Whatever gave you that idea?"

Shielding her mouth with her cup, Judith whispered, "I heard a priest say Rephaiah and Gershom rode out to meet Nehemiah and his party."

Storms brewed in Adah's stomach. She clutched her mother's drink to her belly. "Then a notice did arrive."

Judith took a sip from her cup. "Not to father."

"It will. Next time." Adah kissed her sister's cheek. "And there will be no more tricks. We do not know why the governor came for a visit, but secrets don't stay hidden long. People will gossip."

She had not heard one whisper among the booths in the marketplace as to why a palace official would arrive in Jerusalem. But as sure as she had stood before Nehemiah, the renowned governor of Judah and cupbearer to King Artaxerxes, she would find out why he came to her city. And when she found out the truth, her father and her family would be the first ones to receive her news. Sons or no sons.

2

Adah lay on her back, staring at the ceiling and listening to her sister's soft snores. If only she could find peace in slumber. Gershom's deceit inflamed the layers of her mind like a festering thorn. How dare he keep the governor's letters from her father? And how dare he insult her family? The birth of a daughter was not a curse. Or was it? Her father had no heir, no son to assume his position. Had she let her father down? No. She would not let her thoughts linger in shame. Whatever tasks brought the governor to Jerusalem, she would find them out and help her father get them done.

Sounds. A shuffling noise caught her attention. She listened. Someone scuffled through a front room of the house. Since her father's snore sing-songed across the hall and kept rhythm with Judith's, the late night walker had to be her mother.

Thump. Several soft thuds followed. *The plums.*

Adah banded a linen cloth over her hair in an attempt to tame her wayward curls and hurried to the front of the house. Her mother, dressed for a day in the courtyard, stood near a stack of cups, her hand feeling the table for something solid.

"Mother," Adah whispered. She touched her mother's sleeve. "Morning will not come for several hours. You must rest."

"Oh." Her mother blinked rapidly as her mouth

curved downward in an unhappy smile. "I saw so much light I thought it must be morning."

"Your eyes are deceiving you. Can't you sleep?" Adah knew this was a useless question.

With wide eyes and drumming fingers, her mother looked ready to prepare a feast.

"I will sit in here so as not to disturb your father."

And do what? Blindness eliminated a host of duties. With Gershom's words stuck in her head and now her mother's restlessness keeping her awake, sleep eluded Adah. She might as well breathe in the tepid breeze blowing through the city. Who knows? A new fragrance might bloom in the night. "Why don't we take a stroll?"

Her mother shook her head. "The city can be dangerous."

"Father is known by anyone who may venture out. Besides, no one will chance a crime with the governor in the city." She stroked her mother's arm. "If we take a walk you may grow tired and be able to nap before morning prayer. I certainly cannot sleep after all the festivities." *And insults.*

Her mother gazed into Adah's eyes as if her sight had been restored. "We will not go far."

Adah rounded up the scattered plums and then slipped on a cloak and sandals. She lit a lamp and led her mother to the street. They headed west toward the Valley Gate. With the city wall in ruins, they could saunter as far as they desired.

"What would I do without my daughters?" Her mother's praise held a hint of pity.

Adah squeezed her mother's arm. "You would do just as well with sons."

"They would be snoring alongside your father."

"Like Judith?"

Her mother laughed.

Adah giggled and beheld the stars overhead. Were they brighter in the middle of night? Or did the battered wall and burned gates not compete for their splendor?

A shepherd with lambs as steady on their feet as a sleepy child herded his livestock down a narrow lane. They passed an elderly man carving by moonlight. Near the gate, a few empty barterers' booths faced the road.

Her mother stopped and breathed deep. "Cloves. And pepper. We must be near the merchant's tables."

"We can turn back." Adah laced her fingers in her mother's and gently nudged her arm.

"A little farther. I'd forgotten how the night smells." Her mother's face tipped toward the sky. "We're near a gate. I can smell the charred post."

What remained of the burned-out Valley Gate loomed before them.

No unusual scents piqued Adah's curiosity. "I wish I had inherited your nose."

"You did. The perfume you gave the governor was beautiful." Her mother sighed. "I could smell it on my arm all through the banquet."

"That was chance. And too many tries." Adah shifted a rock from her mother's path. "Maybe one day I will earn your reputation with oils."

Ridges deepened on her mother's brow. Had reminiscing caused her mother pain? Adah's storeroom had once been a thriving business for her mother.

"Do you hear something?" Her mother asked.

Adah scanned the empty marketplace. "I do not

see anyone. A mule is tied to a post. Did he snort?"

Her mother held up a hand and moved her head slowly side to side. "Someone is sobbing." Pointing toward the charred ruins of the gate, her mother whispered, "Over there."

Muffled and staggered crying, came from beyond the city wall.

A cool stream flowed through Adah's veins. What if this person wailed in anger? How could she protect a blind woman?

"We should leave." Adah tugged at her mother's sleeve. "By the time we get home you will be ready to sleep."

"And what of our brother or sister in need? They may be injured. Rubble abounds near the wall." Her mother stepped closer to the noise. "Your father is responsible for the well-being of our people."

"I am aware of his oversight." And she would uphold his honor. Even in the dark. "Stones may have tripped someone. I will see if they are hurt." Her heartbeat drummed a warning at the possibilities of what she might encounter. *Oh, Lord, keep us safe.* "You will stay here. The road is uneven and strewn with pebbles. I cannot lead you and see to another." Or fend off an attack.

"Bless you. I will remain and listen. Perhaps we were restless this night for a reason?"

Yes, because of Gershom's insults and his father's deceit.

She borrowed a crate from a nearby booth and sat her mother on the wooden seat. "Do not wander off until I return. I shouldn't be long."

Her mother nodded. "You have a courageous heart, daughter."

And it had grown in size to fill Adah's chest and throat.

Holding the oil lamp before her, she strolled toward the mournful sounds. If this were a trap, the deceiver would receive a warmed-oil bath. She passed through the remnants of the gate, by a length of crumbling wall, and inched closer to a figure crouched on the ground. Muttered words grew louder. Was this person in prayer or pain? She kept a safe distance in case the stranger lunged.

She licked her lips and concentrated on her single word greeting. "*Shalom.*"

The figure flinched. The weeping halted. No sudden movements came, only a careful rise and a slow turn in her direction.

Her trembling hand held the lamp aloft and sent light gray shadows dancing across a man's face.

"Daughter of Shallum?"

It couldn't be.

"Governor?"

What was the governor of Judah doing weeping outside the city in the middle of the night? Did he find some fault with the officials, or with her father and his duties? And if he had fallen, where were the soldiers that had accompanied him on his trip?

Sweat pooled above her lip as she balanced the lamp. Should she go and find Nehemiah's guard? But where would she look? Her mother waited for her return.

Nehemiah brushed off his robes and swiped at the skin beneath his eyes. No salutation came. Chirping crickets continued their unending song.

"Are you hurt?" She blurted as she scanned his garment for the stain of blood.

He shook his head, but his chest shuddered.

She opened and closed a fist, not knowing what to do or say next. Her wandering alone at night, needed an explanation. A man could scout the streets of Jerusalem in the dark…but not an unescorted girl. And not the daughter of a ruler.

She swallowed, but the lump in her throat remained. A small cough cleared her windpipe. "I did not mean to disturb you, Governor. My mother could not sleep, so I brought her outside for some night air. She heard someone in distress, so I came to see if I could help."

He glanced off into the distance. "Your mother is here?"

"I left her beyond the gate." Would he think her irresponsible? "This section of the city lies within my father's district." She looked around as if a crowd of city dwellers encircled their meeting place. "Most people are known to us."

Nehemiah stepped closer. The flame from the lamp illuminated his finely stitched collar. She lowered the light so as not to irritate his eyes and to show him the respect he deserved.

"You are a brave woman." His praise was filled with the familiar authority she heard at their introduction hours before. "Your compassion knows no end, for you did not turn back at this hour."

If that were only true. Her mother had sent her to seek the mourner. Left to her own decisions, she would have fled. "My mother deserves your praise. She heard you." Heat rushed to Adah's cheeks. "Sometimes I believe God blesses my mother's hearing since her sight is no more."

Nehemiah scrutinized her face as if the sun was in

full glory. "Is her blindness a burden to you?"

"No." Adah flinched at her half-truth and stood a bit straighter.

The governor's stare did not waiver.

"Well, maybe. Some days." Had she ever admitted this truth before? Not desiring to sound hard hearted, she said, "I love my mother. I would never complain about the extra work."

The governor nodded. He averted his gaze and pointed toward some crags in the distance. "My father and his father are buried near here."

She knew the caves of which he spoke, for many tombs were carved out of the same rock.

He continued, "When my brother brought word that Jerusalem wallowed in disrepair, I could not stay away any longer." Nehemiah pressed a fist to his chest as if he were seeing the destruction of his city for the first time. "God has called me to rebuild the birthplace of my fathers. To resurrect the city of His beloved, David." He turned to her with a gleam in his eye. "That, daughter of Shallum, is my burden."

"So that is why you came?" She shifted her lamp. "Not to collect taxes but to set up an office here and bring in workers to rebuild the wall?"

He nodded. "You found me inspecting the wall tonight. The City of David will be a stronghold again." The shadows dancing on his face could not soften his stare, which bore into her gaze like a hammered tent peg. "This wall will rise and these gates will be secured. God has made it clear to me what we must do."

She trusted God. Or at least she had before her mother's eyesight darkened. A year ago she had prayed for a miracle from God for her mother. No healing came. And where was the rain? She had prayed for showers for the fields. Othniel had prayed. Her father had prayed. The soil remained parched. People went hungry. But if Nehemiah had truly heard God's voice, perhaps *Adonai* was showing His favor to His people once again.

"When will the stone masons arrive?" She didn't know much about resurrecting a wall, but the king had renowned craftsmen.

"King Artaxerxes gave me letters for safe passage and a leave from the palace. I have access to the forests in the south. But as for workers, those already living here will secure this city."

Her shoulders sagged. "We have no army. The drought has left families without food and coin—"

"Adah." His address held a tone of chastisement. "Do you believe in God's provision? In answered prayer?"

"Uh, yes." Her answer was not resounding, yet it was true. Once. She rolled back her shoulders and stood soldier straight. Gershom's insult of her family would not stand. "Whatever you need from the household of Shallum, we will provide it for you."

"It blesses my soul to hear that." His tone sounded pleased with her offer, but his crossed arms and cocked head resembled her father when he was none-too-pleased with her actions. "Shall we greet your mother? Then I must rejoin my men." He started toward the gate, indicating for her to lead the way.

Once inside the city, she made her way to her mother's wooden seat and clasped a hand on her mother's shoulder. "Mother, I am not alone."

"Blessings, Elisheba."

"Governor?" Her mother pulled against Adah's

outstretched arm to rise. "I did not expect you to be awake. I sent Adah to check on some noises."

"And she found me. This night snatched sleep from all of us, but now I believe I can rest." He captured her mother's hands in his own. "*Laila Tov.*"

"Goodnight, Governor," her mother echoed.

"And Adah." Nehemiah turned all his regal attention toward her. "What we discussed under the gate shall be a confidence between us. I do not believe our meeting this night was by chance. When I hold an assembly, I expect you to be there."

"Of course." She would stitch her lips together to keep this vow and uphold her family's honor.

Nehemiah nodded and veered eastward.

Her mother fumbled for a hold on Adah's cloak. "Strange to meet the governor at this hour?"

If you only knew. "The festivities of the banquet kept us all up. Now, I believe, I too can sleep."

"Get your rest daughter. For it seems the governor has plans for you."

"You listened?"

"I heard." Her mother patted Adah's arm. "Only his parting instruction."

"I do not see where I can be of much help to him."

"Then you do not have enough faith, for it is not every night the governor of Judah bestows a confidence. You are blessed, my daughter. And you have blessed me more than a son."

Adah stroked her mother's hand. "I will be faithful to God and the governor."

She led her mother home with small steps and a smooth stride. Not one sniffle escaped from the wellspring of emotion tingling behind her eyes and crushing the ribs in her chest. She was not a son, but she meant her vow to Nehemiah. Whatever God asked of her, she would do. Whatever Nehemiah needed, she would make sure the household of Shallum saw to his needs. She could keep a secret, but build a wall? Men would be required for the labor, not women. Gershom's taunts tormented her thoughts. Her father had no sons, no heirs, and no builders.

A rebel tear slid down her cheek. Praise be, her mother could not see her weakness. She fisted the hand not guiding her mother and gazed into the heavens above. A few stars twinkled high above the valley.

Make me able to restore your city, Lord, just like Rephaiah's eight sons.

3

After morning prayer, Adah filled her satchel with ram skin pouches she had washed, dried, and sniffed to make sure no scents lingered. She layered her bag, thickest skins on the bottom, lightest on the top, and hurried toward the outskirts of the city. She did not want to join in public conversations about the governor, for she had promised to keep the reason for his journey a secret. Try as she might to push it to the farthest regions of her mind, the enormity of the task of rebuilding a battered wall haunted her thoughts. How could ruins be resurrected? To keep her mind and mouth from dwelling on Nehemiah's plan, she spent the morning searching for bark, leaves, and rare flowers. Lack of rain hindered her efforts.

On her return home, the stream of travelers stalled outside of the Fish Gate. What was causing this delay on the road? Did fishermen arrive from Joppa with their catch? Her lack of height allowed her to slip ahead of the carts and the curious.

A cluster of men took up a sizeable portion of the path. She recognized one of the route-blockers by his indigo and scarlet robe. The robe he wore to greet Nehemiah.

Gershom flapped his arms like a vulture readying for flight. His finger-jabbing scold lashed out at a few landowners. Othniel's father received the brunt of the attack. Othniel hung back with his brothers. Gatherers pushed her friend closer to Gershom's tirade.

"It is a sin to steal from those in authority." Gershom's hand shot heavenward while his voice carried to the next town.

Adah's heart plummeted to her knees. She wedged herself beside a woman with a wide basket on her shoulder so that she would not be seen. Her father did not rule this part of the city and her presence could add kindling to Gershom's rage.

Othniel's father wrung his hands and then held them up as if he were in bondage. "I have given you a down payment. That is all I can give. Without rain I have no grapes or olives to sell."

Farmers echoed their agreement and roused several passers-by to join in their protest.

Gershom stomped his foot. Clouds of dust floated upward. Did he not see the hopelessness of the drought?

"And what do I tell my father Rephaiah?" Gershom's tone mocked his tenant. "He has been gracious to you for months."

A landowner gestured to the onlookers. "What can we do if the land is empty?"

Weight rested on Adah's shoulder. Had the woman at her side repositioned her basket? The tapping of fingers sent Adah whirling around. Othniel's face was inches from her own. His expression did not hold any of the playfulness she remembered.

Othniel took her hand and turned her eastward toward the next gate. "You should carry on."

"The people's concerns are my concerns. I want to listen." Adah clutched her tunic and willed her heart to steady. She glanced at the basket-carrying woman a few feet away. When had she shifted? If she honored

Othniel's request and left, slipping in and out among the crowd could bring her to Gershom's attention.

She gazed into Othniel's almond-colored eyes and willed hope to spark in them again. Why didn't hard work bring him any gain? If only this were a time for small talk or bantering. She cupped a hand over her forehead so she could see all of his features. His expression remained steadfast. "Besides, the road is blocked ahead."

Gershom clapped his hands to quiet the raucous. "Work harder," he shouted. "The governor's purse cannot be light of taxes."

Disapproval clamored through the crowd.

Othniel surveyed the road and the people. Was he searching for a route out of the masses? He wrung his hands as if he feared a confrontation with Gershom. "You should not witness this anger. I do not want you to worry." He tried to muster a smile as he beheld her face. "My father has a plan to pay his debts to the governor."

"I know your family is trustworthy." Her praise made Othniel stand a bit taller as if sacks of grain had slid from his back. "Your fields are ready for the next rainfall." *Please make it soon, Lord.*

Oh, how she wished she could tell Othniel about why the governor had come to Jerusalem. The truth tingled on her tongue, but she had promised to keep Nehemiah's reason a secret. A simple assurance to ease Othniel's burden would not be a betrayal. On tip toe, she said, "Do not fear, the governor's visit is not about money."

Othniel rubbed his jaw and regarded her as though she had spoken in a foreign tongue. "Then why did he come?"

"Yes, tell us daughter of Shallum, why is the governor here?" Gershom's question invaded her private conversation.

Adah and Othniel rounded on Gershom. Landowners and a host of strangers stared at her as if waiting for the chief priest to read the Law. Her cheeks flamed. Had the sun come to rest above her head covering?

Remember your position. She glanced at Othniel. Feet planted, hands on hips, he reminded her of a pillar. She swung her shoulders back and matched Othniel's authoritative stance. Surveying the faces beholding her as a vision, she smiled, not with false hope, but as a neighbor who truly heard their pleas, and as a woman who would uphold a vow.

"You mistake me for the governor's confidant. I cannot tell you why he is in our city. You went out to greet him. Did he not reveal his purpose?" *Selah!* She had not broken her word to Nehemiah. "You will have to wait upon the assembly."

"Assembly?" Gershom held her gaze captive. "What assembly? The governor has not called for a gathering."

That's right. Nehemiah hadn't called an assembly. Not yet. She licked her lips but her tongue withered like a dried reed.

"It is customary, is it not?" A sideways glance begged Othniel to support her cause.

"The governor should address all of our needs." Othniel waved his hands inciting the people to grumble their discontent.

Gershom yelled at the crowd to quiet. When he turned his attention to her, his face held no patience. He glared at her like a warrior ready to strike. "You are hiding something, or else you came to stir up trouble in my district?"

Before Othniel could challenge Gershom's accusations, she held her arm in front of her friend and kept him penned at her side.

She cleared her throat so her words would carry to everyone who cared to listen. "I have been gathering herbs so I can make perfume and sell it for the poor. Now that I have been detained by your roadside court, the sun is too high for a longer journey." She swiped her tongue over her teeth and prayed for a drop of saliva. "I am no one's advisor, and certainly not the governor's. *Shalom.*"

The hammering of her heart made it difficult to draw her next breath. *Nehemiah, call your assembly soon.* If only the governor knew how much of a burden his secret had become. This bestowing of a confidence had Gershom suspicious, not only of her standing, but of his own.

With a nod toward Othniel, she strode toward the city.

"Of course she runs. She has no authority here." Gershom's insult carried. "And Shallum is too feeble to stroll past the gate."

Adah halted. A flash of fury, hot as a newly stoked furnace, streaked through her veins. She rounded on Gershom. Her arm shot out like a whip with one finger pointed at his upturned nose. She stomped closer to her foe as travelers drew back from her flailing robe and satchel. "Woe to anyone who casts doubt on my father." Her chastisement rose above the rumblings of the people. "So be it if he prefers to do business in private and not like an ox trader in the streets."

A roar of agreement deafened Gershom's

response.

Flinging the fringe of her head covering over her shoulder, she turned toward home and dodged around a wide-eyed Othniel, escaping Gershom's roadside court before the crowd became unruly. After traveling a short distance from the gathering, she ran, and clutched her necklace to her nose, hoping the aroma of sandalwood calmed her trembling hands. The sour stench from her damp palms betrayed her unease at challenging Gershom publicly, but she could not allow her father's rule to be called into question.

When she was almost at the end of the straight street near her home, she slowed and spotted a neighbor struggling with a water jar. A sash hanging from the woman's shoulder bulged over the woman's pregnant belly.

"Beulah, I will assist you." Adah rushed to the expectant mother's side. "Where is your daughter to carry your jug?"

The woman beheld her with scarlet streaked eyes. "My daughter lives in Hebron now."

"Did she marry?" Adah was unaware of a betrothal, but with her care of her own mother it may have gone unnoticed.

Beulah shook her head. "She is a servant in the household of a man who is kin to my husband."

"For how long?" Adah's chest tightened. Water sloshed from the jug she carried. Precious droplets wet her hand.

"Five years." Beulah's words stuttered as she blew out a breath. "They have food and unmarried sons. If she is a hard worker, perhaps one of the sons will offer marriage. With the coins they gave us we can pay our taxes for now."

How could this be? Beulah and her husband lived under her father's oversight. They resided in the district of Shallum, not of Rephaiah. "Did you tell my father of your hardship?"

"He lowered what we owed." Beulah rested her satchel on the threshold of her home. "But it is costly to feed so many." She rubbed her mid-section. "Soon we will have one more."

Adah placed the water jar in front of Beulah's door. She grasped her neighbor's hands and before she could give a reassuring squeeze, the woman clutched her tightly as if verifying Adah was made of flesh and bone.

Breathing became difficult, but Adah embraced her neighbor. "I am sorry your daughter had to leave. I will pray for her well-being."

Beulah softened her grip. "I know you will. I can trust you." She shuffled into her home forgoing any backward glance or farewell.

The pressure mounting behind Adah's eyes pulsed through her face. What was the point of rebuilding Jerusalem's wall if the residents of the city were being sold into servitude elsewhere?

When Adah reached their cooking courtyard, Judith sauntered from the doorway of their home and greeted her in the street.

"We have received our allotment from the governor. Come and see." Judith's lips glistened as she nibbled a honey cake. "Oh, and he has called an assembly for tomorrow at noon."

Toda raba. Only a few more hours to keep Nehemiah's secret.

Guilt seized Adah's stomach as she watched Judith's tongue savor the nectar stuck to her mouth.

She and Judith did not have to struggle to feed their young like Beulah. The governor's provisions kept the household of Shallum from misery and hardship. If only there were enough bags of grain to feed the entire city. Enough rain to grow crops.

But if the people of Jerusalem were faithful and rebuilt the wall at Nehemiah's command, would God's favor rest upon His people again? Would He shower blessings on them? On every single one?

Adah wrapped an arm around her sister. A waft of cinnamon greeted her senses. "We must take our place front and center at this assembly. I want to hear everything the governor has to say."

4

A mass of people, city dwellers, and curious travelers, gathered outside the temple courtyard steps to hear the governor speak. Adah gripped her mother's left arm and led her to the side of the stairs where a two-story dwelling of a temple servant shared its shade with a token few. Judith came along on their right, politely elbowing neighbors who did not take heed of who walked in their midst. Men pushed in closer to the footholds of stone where Nehemiah would make his charge to rebuild the wall.

"Where is the governor standing?" her mother asked.

"On the top step. The rulers, officials, and priests are behind him. Except for Rephaiah who is nearer to the governor." His billowing robe and tall turban nearly blocked the view of the others.

Her mother swayed as if a musician played the lyre. "What is Nehemiah wearing?"

Adah described the indigo robe with gold embroidery and blue ribbing. Elaborate garments rarely graced the streets of Jerusalem except those worn by nobles and rulers. Most people mended their threadbare tunics so they could feed their families or pay a debt with coin instead of children.

The chief priest raised his hand and began to recite the *Shema*.

Joining the prayers of the crowd, Adah echoed,

"Hear O' Israel. The Lord is our God. The Lord alone. Love the Lord your God with all your heart, with all your soul, and with all your might."

Did she? Still love God with all her heart? She glanced at her mother's face tilted toward the sun, her spirit taking flight. How could her mother be at peace with God when He had denied her healing? Why had the petitions for a restoration of her sight been ignored?

"My people." The governor flung his arms wide as if to embrace the crowd.

Nehemiah's greeting turned her attention back to the temple steps. As a child, she listened to the priests sing praises to God for the opportunity to rebuild this place of worship. Sand-colored stone, precisely placed, towered over the landscape of the city. Columns lined the temple building rising from its foundation toward the heavens. Adah prayed Nehemiah's arrival was a balm from God to soothe the hardships of drought and conquests.

"King Artaxerxes is a gracious sovereign," Nehemiah continued. "Our king listened to my concerns regarding Jerusalem, the birthplace of my fathers. My sorrow brought compassion from our sovereign, not wrath." One step. Two steps. Three. The governor paced back and forth. "I have come to set a great task before you. A task blessed not only by the king, but by our God. Shall rodents nest in the rubble-strewn wall of the City of David? Shall we allow this disgrace to continue?"

"No." A battle cry rose above the gathering from every street, alley, and crevice.

"Then rebuild this city with me." Palms open, Nehemiah stretched his arms in the direction of the wall. "Our people rebuilt this temple. We can raise the gates and the wall of Jerusalem. We must be strong and courageous and do God's work. He will not forsake us."

Mutterings grew louder over the gathering until they became a stifled roar.

A man near the stairs called out, "Where are the king's armies? His supplies? Our purses are light."

Nehemiah stared at each section of the crowd with a thin-lipped scowl and with an intensity Adah envisioned of Moses as he held his staff over the Red Sea to part the waters.

"The king has given us lumber for the gates. The rock rests on our soil. Workers are what we need most." The governor stomped his sandaled foot. "We do not need Arabs or Persians to reconstruct this city. The sons and daughters of Jacob can restore the wall. Are you with me? Will Jerusalem rise once more? Or will we leave her in disgrace?"

Adah wanted to join in the jubilant affirmation. Truly, she did. She knew the stories and songs of David slaying his tens of thousands, of his son Solomon imparting wisdom to the whole world, but how was the household of an elderly ruler, his blind wife, and two unmarried daughters, going to restore Jerusalem?

"Will this not lead to war?" a woman asked behind them.

Would it? If this truly was the will of God, who could stand against His people?

Her mother must have heard the question, for her eyes shut and fluttered as if she were caught in a sand storm.

Adah turned toward the gossiping women. "We

must plan for the years ahead. Jerusalem needs a wall to be victorious when a challenge comes. And with the king's blessing on Nehemiah, who would dare wage war on us?"

The naysayer nodded and hastened away.

Returning her attention to her family, Adah smoothed some wayward strands of raven-colored hair from her mother's face. "Father will know what needs to be done to assist the governor."

"At least we are not laborers," Judith said. "We can cook for those who build."

"Cook?" Adah slumped. Was that all Nehemiah needed from her? When he spoke of God's provision that night surely he meant more than food? She had agreed to do whatever the governor asked. Was God finally bestowing a blessing on her city? And if He was, how could she stand idle while others labored? Her stomach cramped, sending an undulating pain across her midsection. *Have I not more to give than warm bread or scented oil?*

A priest rose from his seat in front of the courtyard wall. He clapped and stomped to the edge of the stairs drawing attention to his actions.

"The Levites will repair the Sheep Gate. We will lead our people in toil as in prayer."

And what of Shallum's family? Did her father not oversee half a district? Was her family not as devoted to God?

A merchant named Hassenaah danced on the lowest step. Arms raised, he swayed side to side in a glorious show of support. "My sons and I will restore the glory of the Fish Gate."

The governor stepped forward and held up his hand to cease the cry of volunteers. He ushered a scribe forward and seated him at a long table on the landing above the stairs. While Nehemiah unfurled parchment, the scribe tested his ink and quill on cloth.

Returning to a position in front of the priests, Nehemiah spoke in a booming voice. "The courage of our people will not be forgotten. On this day, we will record the sacrifice and workmanship of all our families for future generations."

The governor acknowledged the people with a continual bob of his head. His gaze beheld each area of the crowd until it rested on her section, her family, and finally on her. Did he remember her promise?

Hassenaah darted to be first in line for the record, but a priest scooted in front of him. Rephaiah motioned for his sons to come forward in haste.

Why should Rephaiah be remembered and not her father? His son Gershom showed no compassion for the poor. Was her father not as devoted to leading the people as any other official? Should his name be banished from the annals because he had no son?

A few women brushed past as they left the assembly. The scent of muted jasmine caught Adah's attention.

"Is it time to leave?" Her mother shifted her weight and leaned on Adah.

Judith tugged at her mother's sleeve. "There is room this way. We are not laborers."

Adah did not budge. A strange buzzing like a persistent horse fly spread from her ears to her thoughts. Wasn't she a daughter of Jacob? Wasn't Judith? Didn't they need to show God that they were as devoted to Him as those stampeding men rushing toward the front?

Judith persisted with her pleas to leave, but Adah

did not loosen her grasp on their mother.

"Wait, sister." Adah's words came out in a rush. "Shouldn't our father and the household of Shallum be in the governor's record? What of our children? Will they not want to see the names of their ancestors and know we were faithful to God's call?"

Her mother tensed. "Your father has no heir."

Judith's eyes narrowed. A scowl puckered her lips. "No one without sons is going forward. What woman would agree to labor with stone?"

A tide pool swirled inside of Adah's belly. Try as she might to remain calm, her ire flared at her family. "Our father, a ruler of this city, sits on a stool hidden by a scribe who will not even ink his name on the parchment. Did Nehemiah not address the daughters of Jacob? Do we not have the strength to pick up a stone?"

Her mother patted Adah's arm. "What makes you think we can do this? We are not craftsmen and we have our own burdens. It is time to lead me home and let the men of this city discuss the labor."

Adah clasped her mother's comforting hand and removed its hold on her body. "You have a daughter to take you home. I intend to restore a section of the wall. God has been deaf to my prayers but perhaps with the governor praying beside me, he will give me the wherewithal to move rock."

Her words were terser than she meant them to be, but they were true and their truth had been bound in her soul for over a year. She pushed through the herd of people trudging forward to heed Nehemiah's call. When she neared the temple steps, she did not take her place in line, but maneuvered past those stoically waiting, ducking under arms and squeezing through slivers of space.

Reaching the platform, she headed toward her father who still sat at the back of it.

Her father stood and surveyed the crowd. "Is your mother well?"

She nodded. "Judith is escorting her home."

Her father rested again on his seat. "Good."

Tell him. Her face flamed as her palms dampened into pools. "Father, your name, our name, should be in this record. Do we not trust God to raise Jerusalem's wall?" *Do I not need to trust Him again? Fully.* She took her father's hand and clutched it between her own. "Help me rebuild our city."

The aged lines on her father's face deepened as if this moment carried the weight of years of grief. "I am too old."

"And I am too young." She lowered to one knee. "Together we can stack stones. Do we not curse them when we stumble?"

"I do." The governor wandered from his post by the scribe with Rephaiah following on his heels. "Your daughter's passion is admirable, Ruler. Do you share the same call to rebuild this city?"

Glancing at the governor, her father said, "If only I had the strength of my youth."

"I know who can give you strength." Nehemiah's gaze did not leave her father's face. "The one who started me on this journey and arranged a foreign king to give me letters to travel. I fasted and prayed and God softened the heart of a sovereign."

Her father rose and drew her to her feet. His forehead furrowed but his eyes gleamed, caging the excitement of a young boy. "Are you certain, Adah?"

Heart fluttering like a homing pigeon readying for

a return trip, she swallowed all her doubts. "Yes, I am certain. If God looks favorably upon us, we can do this."

Rephaiah balked. "The girl knows nothing of masonry. Does she understand the hardship of this task? She has no brothers. Surely, a few of my sons could build Shallum's section. Why should her father be troubled in his advanced age?"

Nehemiah leaned in as if to bestow a confidence on his overseers. "Did David not encourage his son Solomon to be strong and courageous in his attempt to build the temple? Certain battles require strength and courage."

Her father nodded. "May God give me the strength, for my daughter has shown me courage."

A wellspring of warmth surged through her body. Her father had heard her plea.

"But Governor," Rephaiah said. "My sons are strong."

The pounding in Adah's ears resounded like a ceremonial drum. She fixed a stare on Rephaiah that caused priests to step back. Why did this ruler not see that she wanted to be a blessing to her father like his sons were to him? "Did the governor not invite the daughters of Jacob to join in alongside the sons of Jacob? Surely, with God's help, I can build."

"Scribe. Shallum and his daughter will make repairs near the Valley Gate and around the Tower of the Ovens." No one challenged the authority in Nehemiah's tone.

Hushed discord hissed like an asp as it made its way along the line of sons waiting for their names to be recorded on the official parchment.

She assessed the height and width of the earnest

builders as she descended the steps. Could she do the same work? Was pride her folly? From the Temple Mount she glimpsed her city. Rubble could not protect it. A goat could wander in as well as an army.

Casting a hard glance at her skeptics, she said, "We are one man and one daughter, but with God's help, we can set stone upon stone."

"Make that two daughters."

Adah turned.

"And a wife."

Judith and her mother waited arm in arm at the bottom of the steps. Their gold earrings shimmered in the sun.

Adah feared her chest would burst as she gave her best fragrant-blossom smile to her newest stone masons. Who else had builders who wore veils and jewelry? Tears of joy pressed upon her eyes, but she would not let one drop escape.

As she attempted to wade down the stairs to her mother and sister, Gershom stalked after her. Like father, like son.

"You had best rethink this foolishness." Gershom's most holy voice irritated her ears. "My father made a sensible offer. Allow my brothers to build your area. No priest or Levite will oversee a woman in this work."

She rounded on him and jerked her shoulders back. "Are you threatening our religious leaders?"

"I am informing you of reason, woman."

"No, you want to rule alongside your father." There. She said it. The truth. His truth. "You helped my father when my mother was ill, but my father is capable of ruling for a few more years. And the household of Shallum will heed the governor's call."

"Hah. What a sight it will be to see a stubborn hen move rock." He clapped his hands and snickered.

If only she could snap her elbow back into Gershom's belly, but with her mother waiting, beaming with pride, Adah controlled her anger and walked into her mother's outstretched arms.

Her mother tugged her close. "I would much rather have a squawking hen than a braying donkey."

Adah pulled back. "You listened?"

"I heard."

"And then she told me." Judith folded her arms and glared at Gershom. With hair as dark as their mother's, and eyes almost the color of onyx, her twin's stance was formidable.

With hair the color of roasted grain, and cheeks burned by the sun, Adah's scowl could not rival her sister's.

Adah grasped Judith's fisted hand. "But what if no masons come to help us?"

"Did you not hear our governor this day?" Her mother answered. "Be strong and courageous. God will not forsake us. He will provide a mason."

5

The next morning, Adah studied the rows of baked-clay jars stored in a cupboard in her storeroom. The markings on the vessels may as well have been foreign gibberish for as much as her brain was able to concentrate. She had no one to blame but herself for her predicament. The first culprit was her own pride. The second culprit was her own stubbornness. Why did she let them overtake her yesterday? She charged forward and committed to rebuilding the wall with God's help. But where was God? Where was the rain? The abundance of food? The strong backs to lift boulders?

She reached for the mint-scented oil and dabbed a drop on a piece of cloth. The aroma of the crushed leaves usually calmed her spirit. One breath. Rest. A second. She opened her eyes and stood with insides wrapped tighter than a weaver's thread. How was she going to stack stones when she could barely lift them?

She shuffled her jar back and forth over a flat knot in the table's grain. "Lord, I need guidance," she prayed.

"If you rub that bottle any faster it may break."

Adah whipped around at the sound of Othniel's voice.

He leaned against the threshold to her workshop, arms crossed and resting comfortably across his belt.

Had he heard her prayer? She glanced at her hand.

A small tremor unsteadied her fingers.

"I'm mixing oils." *He can see that.*

He strolled closer, his smile as content as a well-fed lamb. "May I?" He held out his hand for the vessel. No dust covered his skin this morning and the curls she spied escaping from under his turban were dark as charcoal. He hadn't been in the fields digging in forsaken soil. Not yet anyway.

She offered him a different jar. "I hope you find this soothing."

He breathed deep. "Ahh. I am in a shady grove with a sea of moss and buds aplenty."

"Will you take me there so I can flee humiliation?"

"You cannot leave." He returned the fragrant mixture to her. "All around the market people are talking about how Shallum and his daughters are going to restore a section of the wall."

Turning slightly toward her wares, she attempted to cap the bottle of tuberose and agar wood oils. Her fingers fumbled the carved poplar cap. Three tries later her mixture was stoppled and set with the others. "I would not doubt King Artaxerxes has heard of my madness."

Her belly cramped. She had volunteered to rebuild the wall so her family would be remembered not ridiculed. She faced Othniel and forced a reluctant grin.

"Come now." His voice calmed her soul more than the mint leaves. "Your father agreed to the work as did your family."

"Alas, I am convincing as well as conniving. My father cannot labor like a young man. I will be the death of him." Her heart beat as swift as the rhythm Othniel drummed on the table. She sighed. "I will speak with Nehemiah today."

"Then he should refuse your appointment." He opened his arms wide as if to embrace her.

She stood as still as a statue.

He stepped closer. "I am here to assist you."

Could God have acted this swiftly in answering her plea? Or was Othniel offering his services out of pity? She shook her head. The gossip muttered among the barterers could not have been kind. Her countenance plummeted like a fisherman's anchor. She rolled her scented cloth until it resembled a twig. As much as she liked Othniel's company, his family needed him to labor in their vineyards.

"I cannot accept your offer. You have responsibilities to your father—"

"And my father sent me to you." He leaned toward her and held out his hands as if he were an offering from his family.

Othniel's skills would be useful. She blew out a breath and tucked her pride away in one of her ram-skin gathering pouches.

"Do not worry." He tipped her chin so she saw nothing but him and everything about him. "My father has five other sons. And you paid too much for the cedar box. I told you it would be noticed."

Her stomach hollowed at his confession and her bones became unsteady at his touch. Or perhaps her senses were finally reacting to the mint. "You're here to pay a debt?"

He dropped his fingers from her face, but the warmth of his skin spread along her jaw and over her cheeks. "I'm here as a friend to the house of Shallum."

"I could use several friends like you." She cleared her throat and tried to hide the giddy smile tugging on her lips. "Lots more. About your height with broad shoulders." She stepped away to place her jars in the cupboard, but her body yearned to stay close and feel his caress anew.

"Hah. You kept it." Othniel came up behind her and reached toward the top shelf of the cupboard. He removed a narrow piece of weathered wood. "Do you remember when we found this?"

"How could I forget? I thought that twig was a live lizard intent on slithering over my foot." Her toes curled at the vision...and from Othniel being near. She spied a few dark hairs peeking out from the opening in his tunic.

He examined the nubs resembling tiny feet. "I knew it couldn't be alive. A skink would run away if it felt the earth move." He held the slim piece of wood in the air and whirled it around like the wooden lizard had suddenly sprouted wings. She stifled a laugh at the amusement their treasure gave him.

"I'm glad you took this home. My brothers would have broken it into pieces." Othniel placed the harmless lizard back on the top shelf and faced it toward her table. "There. Its eyes will watch over you while you create intoxicating perfumes."

She closed the cupboard. "And to think that dirt and creek water created those menacing eyes."

"When we had water." Othniel's voice sounded as rejected as the land.

Adah's mother shuffled into the workshop. "Someone is with you, daughter."

Othniel jumped and nearly knocked over a pitcher of olive oil. Adah caught the handle before it fell. Her mother couldn't see Othniel's closeness with her darkened sight. Adah lived with this knowledge, but

Othniel did not.

"Mother, Othniel is present." She gave Othniel a quick glance and a reassuring nod.

"I thought I heard voices." Her mother scanned the workshop as if sighted. She looked toward where the commotion with the pitcher had occurred. "My daughter doesn't usually talk to herself."

Othniel coughed and shifted further down the table. His carefree expression sobered. "I was coming by the house."

"There is no need. I am here and my husband has gone." Her mother's cheeks plumped with a hint of a grin.

"Othniel has offered to help us build the wall. He is an answer to our prayer." Adah shuffled toward her mother. She would not mention Othniel's obligation to his father or her generous payment for the governor's gift. "Your head band is crooked. Let me fold your veil. We can't have people thinking we are already overworked."

"Why would I be tired when we have so many friends?" Amusement rippled through her mother's words, especially the last one spoken.

Adah tugged her mother's head covering to distract her.

"Growing trees and tilling the soil I can do," Othniel added. "But I have never laid the foundation for a city wall."

"Is there not someone in the governor's party who could give us direction?" Adah asked. Nehemiah had secured lumber, but did he bring advisors?

Her mother's eyes squinted as if pain ricocheted through her temples. "Men with knowledge of masonry will be guiding their own families, but I do know of someone who could assist us."

Assist? Adah needed one of King Artaxerxes's experts.

Reaching for a stool, her mother took a seat. "Telem *ben* Henadad will not be sought by another family. His father was a master builder and helped to rebuild the temple years ago. I was well acquainted with Telem's wife."

"I have not heard of him." Adah swept some dried leaf bits off her mixing table.

Othniel shrugged. "I'm a quick learner." He winked at her. "And one of the few men in Judah who can name flowers. I won't have to name the rocks."

Adah stifled a laugh. Her friend was eager to find laborers. Had God listened to her prayer this morning? Had He sent not only one worker, but two strong men? Her mother's countenance did not overflow with assurance.

Her hope flickered. "Surely someone with Telem's skill will be called upon by others."

"Telem does not reside in the city." Her mother beckoned for Adah's hand and clasped it between her warm palms. "I do not know if he still lives. I once heard he dwelt in the caves north of Jerusalem. Perhaps he will remember me and honor a request from my daughters."

If God was listening to her prayers, He was only lending half an ear. "Mother, we need young men. Not those of father's age."

"He is not aged." Her mother patted Adah's hand. "I can picture his face as if he stood before me inspecting the stones of the temple. He was a mere boy then."

"But a cave?" Adah asked.

"A cave has more protection than our city." Othniel cast Adah a curious look. "If we find this man, will he come to help us?"

Rotating her face toward Othniel's voice, her mother said, "I cannot say for certain. But God has placed Telem on my heart, and I think we should ask him to join our efforts."

Adah withdrew from her mother and began bundling thin strips of cedar to grind for future scents. Oil stains marred the planked wood where she worked. Ovals the color of plums and dates displayed the errors of her past attempts to make perfume. Was it a mistake to waste time searching for a man that may not even be alive? But if Telem did inhabit the caves outside Jerusalem, she could use his skills and spare her family from becoming the laughingstock of the city.

A chill shivered over her flesh as she pictured the darkness of the catacombs. She glanced at Othniel who gave her a slight nod. A surge of renewed purpose flowed through her veins.

Lifting her mother's hand, Adah kissed it. "If it is as you say, and your Telem lives, Othniel and I will find him."

6

Adah halted on a mound overlooking the city. Fields and groves terraced outside of Jerusalem resembled a shroud of burlap with an uneven weave. Shriveled trees and vines rippled across the staggered fields. Lush hillsides were only a memory. For some. She couldn't even recall a bountiful harvest. Today she did not need to search out a lone bloom or young bud, she needed to find a man with the skills to help her family repair their section of the wall.

But could they convince the recluse builder to return? Her mother had been coy about what sent him away. Although she *had* prayed to God for workers, and if this was an answer to her prayer, she would be a fool to refuse it. When it came to her petitions, God's silence had been deafening. Maybe that was about to change?

"Why did I have to come along?" Judith sipped from a waterskin, replaced the top, and slung it over her shoulder. "My legs aren't accustomed to climbing."

Adah bent over and braced her hands on her knees. She breathed deep. "And I don't usually search for plants in caves."

"Maybe we should try." Othniel's forehead wrinkled into a scowl as he scanned the drought-cursed soil. "The lower fields can't even sprout tares."

Uncapping her own waterskin, Adah took a quick drink. "Even up here nothing has caught my eye."

Othniel grinned and stroked his jaw. "Nothing?"

She nearly choked. The gleam in Othniel's eyes sparked a warm flutter in her belly. "Not one leaf." Should she confess her growing fondness for Zipporah's fifth son and work by his side while he repaid a debt?

Judith stared at the incline ahead with a crinkled nose assessment. "How much farther?"

"Until we find our builder or his bones. There are caves at the top of this hill." What she wouldn't give for a whiff of lavender and lily to ease the headache created by all her sister's whining.

Shielding his face, Othniel pointed east. "A branch has been broken this direction." He trudged toward a rocky cliff. "We will begin our search over here."

Adah held out her hand to her sister. "Coming?"

Judith fingered her embroidered head covering and left a streak of dirt behind. "When we reach the entrance, you go inside." Judith crouched on the trail leading down the incline and back to town. "I'll stay out here and keep watch."

Adah followed after Othniel. She wasn't about to force her sister into the cave. A break from the discontent would be a cinnamon balm.

Peeking into the first opening, Adah shouted Telem's name. The darkness echoed her summons. Were they even close to where the man lived?

Othniel emerged from another cave. Hands on his hips, he surveyed the height of the catacombs. "Hiding places abound in these cliffs." He strode toward a fissure in the rocks. "On we go to the next hole."

A flash of shadow banished the sun. Movement near a high boulder caught her attention. "Telem?" The shout of his name scorched her throat. "I am the daughter of Shallum. From Jerusalem."

"Telem. Show yourself." Judith's screech was shrill enough to cause vultures to flee. "I have a stew to prepare. Goat meat with figs await."

"For all her complaining, your sister is showing some wisdom. The offer of food may be our best strategy to lure him out." Othniel braced his hands against a small opening in the cliff. "I am night blind in these pits." Instead of ducking into the rock, Othniel turned toward the path they had climbed. He stilled and stared.

A few heartbeats later, she heard it. Hoof beats. Closing in fast.

Othniel motioned for her and Judith to join him at the cave's opening.

Adah ran and grabbed her sister's hand. "I believe someone heard your summons, but I doubt Telem owns a herd of horses." The catacombs molded into a mass of brown as she tugged Judith toward Othniel. His gesturing was but a blur.

Holding her breath, Adah's heart rallied and drummed in her ears. She became the first to dive into unsurveyed darkness. The tight opening snagged her linen veil, but soon the overhang gave way to an expanse that allowed her to turn and pull Judith through the rock entrance.

Facing the light of day, Othniel shimmied feet first into the cave, whacking the dirt with his turban as if he were under attack.

Our sandal prints. Reaching forward, she placed a hand atop Othniel's curls to keep his head from scraping the tight entry. The wave of his hair was like a silk scarf between her fingers. The softness sent a shiver across her skin. Could her friend fend off these riders if they meant ill? Oh to be back in her workshop in her finger-stained life before Nehemiah arrived in her city.

"Remind me to stay home next time," Judith whispered against her earlobe. "Builder or no builder."

Men's voices echoed in the clearing outside the caves. Had they seen Othniel? Foreign gibberish filled their talk, but a few Hebrew words lingered in their commands.

"We must go deeper," Othniel whispered. He placed her hand on his waist. "Take hold of my tunic."

Adah grasped his coarsely woven garment. What should have been a fitted tunic hung loose. *Curse this drought and famine.*

She gathered the excess cloth. Blinking, she tried to keep her fingers from grazing Othniel's back, but she gently bumped him. Her knuckles rested against his muscular flesh. She would have sworn she stood at a fire's edge. Warmth spread up her arm from where she held onto him.

Othniel stiffened then relaxed.

Judith latched onto Adah's cloak with a talon-sharp grip.

"Not so tight. I must breathe." Adah kept her voice low.

"Who can see in this hole?" Judith loosened her grip.

Holding her hand to his side, Othniel moved forward. "We must ease away from the opening in case a scout ventures inside."

She and Judith plodded in Othniel's wake. Darkness closed in around them as they navigated what seemed to be a tunnel. Adah's arm loosened dirt from one wall as she trudged forward. With her other hand, she felt the coolness of rock. She now knew what it was like to be entombed.

Judith burrowed her head against Adah's back. "If anything crawls on me, I will scream and wake the dead."

Adah shrugged to loosen the pinch of her collar. "I would much rather have a skink slither across my sandal than a strange man touching my dress."

"We may have both," Judith said.

"Shh." Adah blocked the thought from her mind.

Othniel slowed his pace. She heard the tap of his sandal upon the ground testing their route. What she wouldn't barter for a ribbon's width of light. They had fled into a starless expanse of night.

Muffled shouts sounded behind them. Were the foreigners in the cave?

Her skin pimpled and sent a shiver throughout her whole body.

"There is a breeze ahead." Othniel's voice held a hint of hope. "Perhaps there is an opening. We might even have more room to maneuver."

In a few shuffles, cooler air dampened her nostrils. Her chest hungered for more breaths. A strange scent like diluted vinegar hung in the new expanse of cave. Had something died recently? She nestled her face into her head covering and tried to lift her sandalwood and chrysolite beads toward her nose.

"When can we return home?" Judith kept a steady grip on Adah's shoulder. "Surely those men will not venture too deep into these catacombs."

"I don't know." Concern weighed on Othniel's words. "What is there to scout in these hills? The city is unprotected. Who would send riders?"

"Samaritans," a deep voice grumbled.

Adah's heart seemed to loosen from its chamber while Judith slammed into her.

"Telem?" The name flew from her lips like a startled lark.

A mad cackling sent a chill plummeting down her spine.

"You summon me like a dog and now you go silent? What were you expecting? The voice of God?"

At this moment, she would prefer it.

7

They had found Telem, but if this recluse was an ally, why did he not show himself until they were wrapped in total darkness with scouts in pursuit? At least he had answered with a word and not a weapon. When her mother had spoken of Telem, a gentle assurance clung to every remembrance. Adah trusted her mother's wisdom, so for the moment she would trust her mother's mason.

She shushed Telem's raucous laughter. "We are the daughters of Shallum. Our mother Elisheba sent us to find you." Adah babbled to the ceiling, for Telem's voice echoed above all of their heads.

"What could an official's wife need with me? I have not resided in the city for years."

"Some help." Judith's voice was but a squeak.

"Your stone craft." Othniel spoke as if this were common knowledge.

"Both." Adah swallowed to provide her parched throat with an oasis of water. "The governor of Judah has petitioned the people to rebuild the wall of the city. My father has no sons to labor on our section. He has two daughters. We need your expertise to rebuild and also to find a way out of this cave."

"Nehemiah is here?" Telem asked.

Was Telem ignoring their plight? "Yes, the governor arrived with the king's cavalry a few days ago."

Telem scuffed closer. "Then that explains why those half-breeds scout the city. They are threatened by the governor's arrival."

Othniel's head shook. "Nehemiah did not bring an army to fight all of Samaria. He has a small escort."

"Doesn't matter—"

Rocks skittered along the path they had recently traveled.

"Can you run?" Telem's inquiry was close to her ear.

"Yes," she and Judith answered in unison.

Othniel stepped in front of her and Judith, guarding them like a sentry. "We will hurry after you."

"The path ahead is well traveled," Telem said. "Trust your footing and stay close."

Adah trailed after Othniel, nearly breaking into a run, her hand practically stitched to his garment. Judith's grip was a constant vice on Adah's shoulder. How could Telem see to bank left and right in pure darkness? His form was almost a vapor. Adah blinked, but her eyes were useless.

When they finally stopped, Adah's chest heaved for want of air. "Are we safe?" She exhaled.

"No one will find us now. And if they light a torch, bats will swarm them."

Telem's confidence calmed her worries.

Judith's forehead rested upon Adah's shoulder. "Did he say bats?"

"Do not think about the rodents. Be strong and courageous." Adah stroked her sister's hand. This darkness was no different than the black abyss their mother lived in every day. They would emerge from this gloomy cave soon enough.

"Are these the only foreigners you've seen?"

Othniel asked.

"Besides you?" Telem chuckled.

Adah did not laugh at their guide's humor. Her knees grew unsteady at the thought of meeting soldiers. "We are not foreigners."

"True." Telem's tone sobered. "I do not see many men in these hills. A bandit or two. But if the governor is serious about fortifying the city, other enemies will come."

Warmth flooded her cheeks. How could this recluse question Nehemiah's determination? She had seen the cupbearer weeping over the wall. "The governor is steadfast. Timber from the king's forests has been arranged and Nehemiah has been granted a leave of his duties at the palace. Families have committed to rebuild sections of the wall."

"That is why we seek you." Othniel's charge held no hint of their dire need.

Telem scoffed. "I am no relation."

"No you are not, but my mother spoke highly of you." Adah swore the thump of her heart could be heard in town. She prayed Telem would honor her request for she needed his skills to uphold her oath to Nehemiah, to her people, and to her God. "Why would an official's wife send us to you if you could not help?"

"I can only guess." Telem's tone was as dull as the rock he hid under.

"My mother saw you in a dream, a vision. She said you owe her a debt."

"Why else would we be in this pungent tomb," Judith snapped.

Adah's chest burned as if she had forgotten to breathe. "I know my mother. She would not have sent us if she did not believe you would honor her request.

Bevakasha, please come with us. My father is old. My mother is blind. We are young and emboldened, but we have never built anything. Not a wall that can withstand war."

Nothing came forth. No explanation. No assurance. No excuse.

"Leave him," Othniel snapped. "He prefers to wallow in filth."

Was there ever a time Othniel hurled curses? She could not remember an incident.

Othniel stiffened under her touch. "Will you at least assist me in escorting the women back to the city?"

Back to Jerusalem? This couldn't be the end. She needed Telem's expertise. She had come all this way upon her mother's urging because God had sent a vision. Or a thought. Or something. What would she do without a master builder?

Adah's chest tightened, but not from Judith's pull on her cloak. Darkness shrouded her desperation. For once, not being able to be seen wasn't a curse.

An odd clicking noise came from where Telem hid. "I've numbered more than a dozen men. We cannot go out the way we came."

"Isn't there another way?" Her voice was too high pitched even for her own ears. "Do these caves join together or something?" *Anything?* Tiny sparks blurred Adah's impaired vision. How would she get Judith home? And Othniel?

"You may thank the Jebusites, daughters of Shallum, for they built tunnels under the city that allowed David and his fighting men into the bowels of Jerusalem. This one goes just north of the main gate before it collapses."

Praise God. "My mother will fret if we're delayed past night fall."

Judith gave a weary sigh. "How long is this journey to freedom? I am covered in dirt."

Shuffling noises came from where Telem loomed. "Then I will light a lamp to carry."

"You're only doing that now?" Othniel's huff sounded like a storm wind.

"We were too close to the opening before. Should I have invited the bandits in for some wine?" Telem made striking noises.

"The lamp will not draw creatures?" Judith fluttered a hand above their heads as if they were already under siege.

"We won't carry an open flame." Telem chuckled.

Trying to diffuse tension and keep in Telem's hospitable graces, Adah asked, "Where do you get the oil for the lamp?"

Clitch, clitch. "I trade."

"With what?" She hadn't seen jugs or vessels in the cave.

"Meat."

Judith wrapped her arm around Adah's waist with a force that could have burst her waterskin.

A small blaze erupted in the tunnel. Flames consumed dried grass.

Finally some light.

Adah clamped her eyes shut from the brightness and slowly opened them. Her guide, mason—this stranger—crouched on the tunnel's dirt floor, his hair dangling awfully near the embers. His face was shrouded by his mane. The lamp wick sucked in the fire. Telem stomped on the smoldering grass and then held the oil lamp high.

Was Telem a man or a beast? She would have sworn he peeked from under a bramble bush. Telem stood a hand taller than Othniel and, from the looks of the man's tunic, he may have bartered for oil, but he didn't own a wash basin.

Othniel stepped backward pressing Adah and Judith closer to the cave's wall.

Telem regarded Othniel with interest. He smirked at his young challenger.

She blinked at Telem and tried to behold him in the dim halo of light that banished the dark. The scent of fire pit ash irritated her nose. With a nod, she tried to show respect to the man her mother recalled with fondness.

Judith peered around Adah's loosened veil, still gripping her sister like a vice. No complaint came about being the one farthest from their host and wedged against juts of dirt and clay.

Telem gasped. "Tabitha!" He leapt like a startled lion, dodging Othniel, and closing in on Judith. "Elisheba has returned you to me." He stared dumbstruck at her sister like he beheld a medium's ghost.

Adah straightened. Her heart may have broken a rib, for pain shot through her chest. "This is my twin sister, Judith. Oldest daughter of Shallum."

"'Tis true." Judith's voice warbled. "I do not know a Tabitha."

Telem's gaze intensified.

Othniel grasped Telem's wrist. "Show us the way to Jerusalem, or give us the lantern and let us be on our way."

Adah fisted her hands. Size of a beast or not, this man would not harm her sister.

"Truly." Judith recoiled further from Telem. "I am not your Tabitha."

Telem stepped backward, cradling the lamp to his chest and mumbling words Adah could not decipher. In a stupor, he swaggered down the tunnel on the way to what Adah hoped was the city.

What haunted this man? And why did her mother send them to find him? Was this a work of God or foolishness?

Othniel turned to them, eyes wide. "If he tries anything, I will detain him. Run back the way we came."

"Bandits or a crazed recluse?" Judith's words were barely audible. "Do we have another choice?"

Adah's temples pulsed. Did she trust her mother's intuition about Telem? Did she trust her own? She grabbed her sister's hand. "I do not believe this man to be dangerous. Seeing you nearly brought him to tears."

Judith tilted her head. "I could say the same."

Adah marched after Othniel, who trailed Telem at a distance. Her feet ached for a rest, but she would not stop until she saw the sun set high over the temple. Not two words were uttered by their leader. He remained speechless on their journey. Telem lumbered through the tunnel like a complacent bear, dodging low hanging ceilings and boulders without a misstep.

Why did he seclude himself in these caves? He did not seem mad. He caught game and traded for his needs. He conversed in Hebrew and understood a foreign tongue. Was this Tabitha to blame for his isolation?

They followed Telem's determined stride until rays of light from an opening in the ground shone into the darkness. Adah would have sworn an angel hovered above the tunnel. Oh, if that were true and a legion of God's messengers waited to right the wall.

Telem squinted into the sun. "I will give you a foothold so you can climb out."

Othniel shouldered past their guide. "I will go first in case those scouts ventured closer to the city." He cast a glance at her and Judith for a silent approval.

She nodded.

"As you wish." Telem laced his fingers and, as soon as Othniel balanced himself on one sandal, Telem thrust him upward.

Othniel grabbed hold of the ground and scrambled through the hole. In an instant, he reappeared and watched Telem's every move. "Send the girls up."

Judith raced forward, dug her sandal into Telem's palms and reached for Othniel's hand as if it were made of gold.

Telem hesitated.

"Push me up," Judith demanded. Her onyx-eyed glare bore into Telem.

Adah cleared her throat. Telem eased Judith toward Othniel as if she were a fine alabaster vase.

Once her sister was safely above the tunnel, Adah faced Telem. Desperation crept over her like an infectious rash. How could Telem refuse to return to his own city? Where was his loyalty to Jerusalem? To her mother? She had agreed to set stone upon stone, and she would uphold her vow, with or without Telem.

She whipped her head back and met the stare of the wayward Israelite. "What shall I tell my mother? Does she not matter to you? Did she ever?"

Telem's lips became as thin as thread. He shook

his mane. "Maybe you should ask her why she tried to trick me by sending a daughter into my presence that resembles my wife."

How dare he insult her mother? *Wife?* No woman lived here. Heat flashed through Adah's body from her toes to her temples. Did this man not listen?

"My mother is without sight." The statement flew loud and fast from her lips. "She has not seen her daughter's face in more than a year. If anyone is a trickster it is you, Master Builder, creeping around in your cave."

"Adah." Othniel encouraged her to grab his hand.

She waved off her friend. Telem went rigid like a statue with eyes. "Our God has given the governor the resources to rebuild Jerusalem's wall. I for one, will answer the call no matter if I break my back doing it. Go ahead and hide out here in your hole. Maybe you'll find your Tabitha."

Telem yanked her close. Every bone and muscle in her body tensed.

"Go ahead," she said. "Betray me and my mother. But how will you explain your betrayal to God."

He placed his hands on her hips and thrust her toward Othniel's waiting arms. The force of Telem's push and Othniel's pull, sent her crashing to the ground.

Othniel knelt beside her. "Are you hurt?"

She didn't answer. She half-crawled, half-ran to the opening. Telem would not treat a daughter of Shallum this way.

The tunnel stood empty. Telem was gone, along with her hopes of having a skilled craftsman lead her team and uphold her family's reputation. Remembering Nehemiah's challenge from the words of

David, she yelled into the pit, "Be strong and courageous and do the work. Do not be afraid or discouraged for the Lord, God is with us." She turned and caught Othniel and Judith staring at her as if she had heat sickness.

Adah sprang to her feet, dusted off her dress, and adjusted the beads of her necklace. "I tell you the truth," she said, a fist resting on each hip. "With or without Telem's help, Jerusalem's wall will rise again."

8

Days later, Adah perched atop a stone as the sun sank below the distant hills leaving a haze of muted scarlet at the sky's edge. Without Telem, a shoulder-high column erected with a few squared stones was all her family had managed to build. Her palms ached like she cradled the setting sun. Every finger had a blister at its base. Did she have the strength to struggle through another day?

"God, where are You in my need? My body is weary. What strength do I have compared to a man?" A warmth tingled behind her eyes. "Was it a mistake to step forward and heed the governor's call?"

The shuffling sound of sandals grew closer. Was one more gawker coming to laugh at the daughter of Jacob? A woman foolish enough to do a man's work.

"It is getting late." Othniel climbed onto her rock, balancing with one arm as he steadied a basket with the other. "Your mother is worried. She sent me with some bread and oil."

Adah took the food while Othniel settled next to her. "I told her I would be along, but I believe my feet are baked onto these boulders. I cannot take one more step."

She uncapped the bottle of oil and breathed in the aroma of lavender and iris with a hint of bay leaf. The sweet, herbal scent renewed her spirit. She handed the small jar to Othniel, rose from her seat, and walked to a vessel of water to clean her hands. "Blessings upon my mother for sending a soothing balm. She must be concerned."

Othniel turned toward her. He waved the bottle under his nose and breathed in the fragrance. "Your family saw how hard you worked."

Adah dried her hands on a cloth and returned to her spot next to Othniel. "Yet everyone has completed double of what we have done."

"Is this a race?" Othniel broke off a piece of bread and offered it to her.

"I wish it were, so it would be over by now." She bit into it. A rush of rosemary and garlic awakened her tongue. "Judith has added some herbs."

Othniel grinned at her with a face scrubbed clean of the day's dirt. "Your sister blends spices I have never heard of before, but then I have never been to the palace in Susa or eaten of the governor's provisions."

The seasoned bread became a lump of dough in her stomach. She could not remember a time when Othniel had eaten at her family's table. So many people suffered from hunger and debt. How could she complain about a few calluses? *Look around you.*

While she ate, Othniel surveyed the scattered stones and told her which ones would be best for the base of the wall. His words grew in eagerness as her heart grew in sadness. Would Othniel's reputation be sullied for working with her? Would his brothers tease him when the height of the woman's wall lagged behind all others? Was it fair of her to hold him to his pledge? Later she would deliver meat and spices from her father's rations to Othniel's household to ward off any grumbling from his brothers.

A bite of bread stuck in her throat. She coughed

and forced a subdued enthusiasm. "Have you checked on your family's progress?"

He shook his head. A few unruly curls strayed from beneath his clean turban. "I work for you."

"You mean you work with me. I paid you with my father's coins."

"But I took them from your hand, and we will honor our commitment to the governor and to God. Speaking of hands." He took hold of her right one. "Where is that oil?"

She tried to pull free from his grasp but his grip did not lessen. Another quick tug. "What are you doing?"

"Healing these blisters."

Othniel held onto her hand, but he managed to uncork the balm. Her insides rolled as if they were swept upon a wave, for his touch was firm yet gentle enough not to irritate her sores.

"My skin is accustomed to tilling hard soil." He cocked his head. "When was the last time you farmed?"

Wiggling her toes, she tried to concentrate on another part of her body other than the one Othniel stroked. "I don't believe I have ever tilled a field...unless digging a root is counted."

He laughed. "It isn't."

She let him turn her palm toward the darkening sky. A drop of oil stung her raw flesh ever so slightly, but it was a good sting like one that would end in healing. Othniel's thumb caressed the joints in her hand, round and round, weaving a pattern across her skin. If the wind blew her off this rock she wouldn't even care, for the aroma of sweet lavender and Othniel's careful touch had caged her will to fight his closeness.

"You shouldn't be doing this." Her wisp of discouragement fell on mute ears, for when he reached for her other hand she gave it freely.

"I know what I am doing." His gaze held her attention like an enchanter's spell. "I'm applying a balm to a fellow laborer's hand. Who is going to challenge me?"

"I am."

Adah gasped, pulled her hand from Othniel, and slid from the rock to face the rebuker. Her heart fluttered to her throat, banishing her moment's rest. The basket of bread tumbled to the ground as Othniel drew to her side.

"Telem?" Her voice rasped with disbelief. The recluse stared at her, a donkey at his side. His hair was tied at his neck with only a hint of the bushiness remaining. His twisted yarn of a beard had been cut short. Telem's woven tunic showed no signs of wear and he was flanked on each side by young men of some means who carried thick satchels. If she didn't recognize his deep boom of a voice, she would have strolled right by him on the street. "What are you doing here?"

Telem clicked his tongue. "Did you not summon me to restore your section of the wall, or was your arrival in my cave a dream? Oh no, it couldn't have been, for I remember the foreigners traipsing through my home." He hooked a thumb in his corded belt. "Though you seem to have forgotten the threat, for we strolled right through Jerusalem's gates."

A surge of energy almost lifted Adah off the ground. How dare Telem toss her through a hole in the ground and pretend he was the one who was wronged.

"We did tell Nehemiah about the scouts in the hills," she said. "The governor has letters of travel from the king and showed them throughout Hauran and Samaria for safe passage. Our city officials believed the men to be curious, but not a threat. No one has ventured into the city."

"Hah." Telem's outburst sent his donkey into a backward side-step. "Since when did a piece of parchment keep the enemies of Judah from conspiring against us?"

She squeezed the handle of her basket with such fervor, her palm flamed. She contemplated tossing the woven carrier at Telem. "Are you questioning my father's judgment?"

"Someone should." Telem regarded Othniel. "Do not tell me you trust half-breed Ammonites and Samaritans?"

Othniel kicked at the ground with his sandal. He cast a glance her direction. "We are under the king's protection."

"And which one of our corpses is going to alert Artaxerxes about a surprise raid?" Telem nudged one of his companions for affirmation.

Did Telem think she was ignorant of the threats Jerusalem faced? Had she not heard stories of Nebuchadnezzar's siege? Seen the rubble from the destruction of her city? Heard of the scattering of her people?

She wrapped her arms around her waist to keep her hands from trembling. "Jerusalem has enough rulers to see to her safety. Meshullam's daughter would have sent word if her father-in-law was bringing soldiers from beyond the Jordan to wage war on Jerusalem. Meshullam is restoring our city's wall not far from our site. He is loyal to Nehemiah."

Telem threw up his hands. "Who discusses battle plans with a woman?" His gaze darted between her and Othniel. "Seek out Nehemiah again. That is all I ask."

"And what about your masonry skills?" She threw her shoulders back. A dull ache greeted her straightened posture. "My task has not changed. I mean to restore a section of this wall so no enemy will be too great for my city."

"So you said in the cave." Telem grabbed a sack from atop his donkey. The two men accompanying the builder looked like they had been struck dumb. "There is no need to repeat your request. We have come to aid you."

Adah breathed out the angst of the past days. She now had a skilled mason to guide her family and more helpers with strong backs. *Selah!* God had not abandoned her in her pledge.

She nodded toward Telem and his men and tried to subdue her exuberant spirit. Perhaps with expert workers, her section would rise past the others. "Then we welcome you."

Othniel positioned himself at her side. "Greetings my brother, even though your assistance comes later than we expected."

Telem splayed an arm over his packed donkey. "How could I run off without my belongings or my tools?"

Telem gave orders to start a fire. One of his men grabbed a shovel and headed toward the stones upon which she and Othniel had been sitting.

Othniel took hold of the donkey's bridle. "It's almost dark. We have finished for now."

While inspecting their wall, Telem paused. "You may work the middle of the night or the middle of the day. Your choice. But this work is not done."

"Of course not." Adah followed Telem outside the wall. "It has only been a few days since we visited you in the catacombs."

"The cornerstone is too small." Telem pointed to the cut stone they laid. "Do you want an easy breech?" He kicked at the next boulder. "Who leveled the ground? I can pound a foot under here."

Othniel scaled over the stones waiting to be placed. "What are you saying?"

"He's saying we need to start anew." Adah's throat tightened. She barely had the energy to remain upright, but she had pledged to complete a section of the wall, and finish this section she would.

Flames erupted from a fire pit near where she and Othniel had sat. How foolish they were to be content with their own unskilled labors.

She glanced up at the graying sky. A few stars shone overhead. One hovered so close above the temple, it appeared a priest could touch it on his tip-toes. Breathing in the scent of the campfire, she closed her eyes and imagined what Jerusalem would look like with a barrier enclosing its homes, markets, and streets. Streets where King David danced and warriors died.

When she opened her eyes, she turned toward Telem. "Find our cornerstone, mason. Let's make Jerusalem a fortress once again."

9

After the Sabbath, Adah devoted herself to laying the foundation for her family's section of the wall. Priests labored near the Valley Gate, so her father's area would need to abut their build. She tugged on the bridle of Telem's donkey, her arm muscles tensing as she coaxed the animal forward and up an embankment. The large rock harnessed to the donkey would add width to the base of the wall. Othniel dislodged the stone for momentum so the animal would not balk at the weight as it pulled the stone up the slow rise of the valley.

A faint ache pulsed through her healing blisters as she guided the donkey closer to the stone cutters.

Telem halted his shaping of the stone and stood, arching his back with his blade overhead for balance. "Where did you go to get that boulder? The palace in Susa?"

"I do not want the donkey to go lame." She patted the animal's neck. Damp hair clung to the bandage on her blistered hand. "He needs a rest soon."

"The donkey or the boy?" Telem chuckled and aimed his blade toward Othniel.

Othniel gave the large stone a shove. "If the animal goes down, we will carry these loads with our backs." He wiped his brow and cast a glance at their task master. "I am accustomed to clearing fields of rocks. You only lived in one."

"Hurry then, teacher." Telem grinned while hammering a newly placed stone. With each strike hair escaped from its band. "We need to cut another rock."

Othniel jogged alongside the boulder as it slid on smoothed ground. "Did someone not feed our mason this morning? He is snapping more than a turtle."

Adah placed a finger to her lips. "Judith keeps his stomach full. He must be getting hungry."

She neared the work area that had doubled in size since Telem's arrival. In the center of the cleared ground, ended by the collapsed wall and a row of dwellings inhabited by the relatives of priests, stood a pot cooking over a flame. The air smelled like pine sap, but Telem assured her that she was mistaken about his mixture. A mortar barrel set beside a row of water jugs. Crushed limestone speckled the dirt.

Her arms trembled from battling the donkey's stubbornness. A fresh spot of blood stained the cloth protecting her palm, but she would not complain. A swell of gratitude pounded through her chest. How could she thank God for providing a mason and laborers to assist her family?

Not only did Telem return to his birthplace, but he brought two brothers with him, Jehu and Jehuliel. These brothers, returning from Sidon, had joined Telem on his trip from the hills. While Jehu and Jehuliel cut stone, Telem fastened the bricks together with the tiniest of seams. Her father carried buckets of sand instead of passing judgment in the courts. And now, younger men lifted rock instead of an old man and his daughters. The clanks and scrapes of chisels, mallets, and blades created a rhythm more melodious than a finely plucked harp.

As far as she could see, her people labored to

restore dignity and protection to their city. Dust clouds rose from where stones were shaped. Smoke escaped from beneath boiling pots. Jerusalem would once again be the sparkling jewel of Judah. What a proud governor they would have in Nehemiah.

Othniel stroked the donkey's muzzle, pleasing the animal. "Your sister and mother are coming with food for the beast."

His teasing broke her trance. "The donkey or Telem?"

"*Shalom.*" Adah waved. Her mother approached carrying a large basket while Judith balanced a jug on her shoulder and took hold of their mother's arm.

Turning his back toward the workers, Othniel leaned in as if to check the donkey's bit. "Did your mother reveal what happened to Telem's wife? For it appears he may seek another." He nodded in Judith's direction.

"Woe to the thought." She admired Judith's scarlet veil and braided belt. If the ensemble caught Adah's attention, a man's eye would surely be drawn to her form. "My mother said it wasn't her place to speak of Telem's past. The truth should come from him."

The reclusive and stiff-necked mason practically leapt from his station on the wall as her sister grew near. Telem tossed his mallet to the ground without seeming to care where it landed.

Othniel patted the donkey's shoulder. "Will you share the truth with me when it is revealed?"

"What don't I share with you?" Othniel had been at her side listening to her babble as they accompanied her mother all over the outskirts of the city seeking plants for fragrant oils. He knew the valleys and streams and, during the last year when her mother stayed indoors, they had traveled the terrain alone.

"Good. Then we agree." He grinned as if he already harbored the secret. "Now I am going to see what is in that basket your mother is carrying."

"Save a bite for me. I will see to our beast." Adah led the donkey to a small trough for a drink. She smiled as the animal submerged its nose and snorted.

If anyone deserved to hear the truth about Telem, it should be her friend. Othniel had escorted her and Judith into the dark catacombs and risked his life returning them to the city. Thinking about her closeness to Othniel's muscular body as they trudged through the shadows heated her cheeks faster than a hot bath. She shook the vision from her mind. *Stop it. You have a wall to build.*

Adah hung back as the laborers washed their hands and claimed bread, dates, and raisin cakes from her mother's noonday offering. Judith poured cups of water to refresh the men. Her sister stood beside the crumbling corner of a house abandoned since the Babylonian siege. Would the owners ever return?

Seeing the progress all around the city gave Adah a sense of pride in her people and in her mission. Like small ants carrying a large crumb, her people heeded Nehemiah's call.

She scaled an expanse of wall above the cornerstone resembling a staircase to the sky. With her family distracted, she climbed onto the rock that had caused Telem and Jehu to grunt like hogs as they set it into place. She tapped the surface three times with her sandal before scaling the stone. The mortar did not bulge. Rising to the heights of two-storied dwellings, she stationed her feet on the stone she and Othniel had pulled up the ravine. She tapped her foot again, confident this section of the wall would rival any other. Perched high above the city, she scanned the uneven rooftops, the scarred walls from one too many siege, and her people rushing through chores.

Othniel came and sat at the base of her tower. He nibbled on the sweet bits of fruit in his cake. When was the last time he had enjoyed such a delicacy?

Holding a plump date between his fingers, Othniel smacked his lips together. "You should snatch a morsel before Telem devours the woven reeds of the basket."

"Where is your faith in my sister's resourcefulness?" She leaned forward and watched Othniel savor his date. "Judith will save me a cake lest I insist she carry stones."

Shading her face, Adah surveyed the hills where they had found Telem. When the wall was finished it would hide the low lying mounds, acacia trees, and bramble bushes from view. In the distance, the soil moved. She squinted. Had she been in the sun too long? Was the heat plaguing her sight? Her skin tingled. No, this was not the sun's deception. Travelers to Jerusalem did not come in such a mass. Not from the west, and not heading toward the devastation where Nehemiah wept. An army descended upon the city.

"Soldiers," she shrieked as panic rose in her soul. Adah turned and dropped to her knees, glancing at Othniel before fixing her gaze on her father. "Soldiers are advancing toward the city. The valley is filled with men."

Adah retraced her trail on the makeshift stairs. Her heartbeat boomed in her ears, loud enough to deafen the commands spewed by all in range of her alarm. How could they fend off a well-planned attack? The wall around the city was not yet half built and some areas even lacked a foundation. Who would war against Jerusalem when the governor resided in its midst? Nehemiah had a commission from the king.

A trumpet blast echoed over the streets of the city. Someone else had spied the enemy. She shivered as if God had finally sent a cool rain over the stricken land.

A boy ran past, his scream a higher pitch than the ram's horn.

"Grab your swords. We must fight," the boy shouted.

Othniel grasped her hand. "Take your mother home and stay there." His words raced faster than the messenger.

She resisted his tug. "This is my city and my wall." Her stomach cramped at the thought of losing everything she held dear. "No one will breech it without meeting my wrath."

Othniel released his hold and picked up a cutting blade. "Not before they meet mine."

10

Adah left her mother in the care of Judith and a servant, and hurried down the street with her father's robe, cloak, and sword bundled in her arms. Her own small blade stayed hidden in her sashed belt while her pouch of sling stones bounced and accosted her hip. Rounding the corner of an alley not far from her home, she found Beulah with her arms outstretched as if to greet those passing by. Her pregnant belly was a roadblock to the men racing to face the enemy.

With a slight adjustment, Adah held her father's possessions in one arm, and freed a hand to hold off her neighbor's charge. She yearned to give some fleeting comfort to her neighbor. Adah's chest cinched at her friend's grief. "Beulah, we must get you out of this stampede."

"My husband and sons are braving the southern rubble. My daughter is gone. Am I to be left alone with my babe?"

"Stay with my mother and Judith. Pray to God for the city." Adah held Beulah's tear-filled gaze, hoping the woman heard the determination in her plea and ignored the trembling of her hand. "You must be brave. God will act."

"Why is it taking Him so long?" Beulah's staggered breaths shook her tattered collar.

A vision of Beulah's daughter smiling gap-toothed and threshing with her mother clouded Adah's thoughts and seized her heart.

"Sometimes God stays silent. I don't know why." Adah stroked Beulah's cheek. "I must go now. Judith will have something prepared to settle your woes."

Breaking free, Adah sprinted to where her father waited in laborer's rags, trying to convince enemy army commanders of his importance. She raced by archers climbing to the tops of buildings and priests ordering families where to fight. An ever present *scritch* of a grinder's stone sharpening swords gnawed at her nerves. The eerie scratch settled in her ear like the irritating sound of a mosquito.

No eye would miss the governor of Judah sitting high on a stallion draped in the vibrant scarlet and golden colors of the king. A few feet outside the Valley Gate, two of Artaxerxes' cavalry flanked Nehemiah's side with armor polished to tempt a thief.

The rulers of Jerusalem sat on donkeys not far from the splendor of the king's warriors, but remained partially hidden behind short towers of stones. Ezra, an elder priest, and a small group of temple servants remained on alert, stationed behind newly constructed sections of wall.

Enemies of her people lay in wait behind terebinth and oak trees, spread out to the north. A formation of soldiers with shields hung back from the rubble of the former fortified wall.

But wait. What was Gershom doing seated at his father's side? Why did Rephaiah's son deserve a mount? He did nothing but stir up angst among the landowners.

"*Abba*," she called as she passed between rows of familiar faces. Faces of merchants, farmers, silversmiths, and sons ready to kill whatever evil invaded their city.

Her father dismounted. "Place my robe over this tunic. I cannot leave my position."

Rephaiah coughed. "For now at least you have your daughter doing something befitting a woman."

Gershom smirked. "More like a servant."

Pressing her lips together, Adah withheld a rebuke. Her father had enough troubles. She would not stir up another.

Shallum turned and slung his shoulders backward. His stance drew her posture to new heights. She struggled to drape and secure her father's gold-banded turban.

"Whatever my daughter does is befitting a woman of stature." Her father's rebuttal echoed over Jerusalem's fighting men. She pretended the attention garnered by an official's pronouncement focused on the lines of troops facing the city rather than the lone woman at the front of a battle. Pride burst through her rib cage at her father's defense.

She fumbled the last cinch of her father's belt. Row upon row of foreigners waited in the fields she had scoured for buds and roots. Her gaze settled on the lead rider. She recognized the crooked-nosed governor trotting on his horse in front of his fighting men. Years before, she had seen him in the city. He held her interest as she wondered how, and if, he could smell with such a disfigured nose. Especially when it was tilted so high and mighty.

"Why is the governor of Samaria challenging our city?" She assisted her father as he remounted. "Did Nehemiah not cross through his lands to Bethel? Our governor has orders from Artaxerxes."

"It seems not even letters from the king can keep

our neighbors from sniffing around our wall." Her father sat straight in the saddle as if King David himself flanked the officials of his city. At least the work that had been completed in the last days cast shade on the men standing guard inside the battered gate.

Reaching up, she wiped a smudge from her father's cheek. "God stands with us. He sent Nehemiah to rebuild our city and He will end Sanballat's trickery." *Oh Lord, may this be Sanballat's end and not ours.*

Her father urged his donkey forward and stood even with Rephaiah, not far from the men taking cover in the ruins. She hid behind a six-foot tower of stones Telem had fit together.

A tap upon her shoulder diverted her attention from the regal rulers of Jerusalem. She turned and beheld Othniel. His ridged forehead and the firm grip on her sleeve betrayed his intentions.

"These men seek a battle, and if we honor their request there will be bloodshed."

"I did not come unprepared." Her reflection filled the amber ring in his light brown eyes. "I have a knife and sling stones under my wrap."

He shook his head and withdrew his hand from her garment. "Death or captivity will come if our men are routed. You must be prepared to escape."

"And how do I do that with warriors guarding the outskirts? I prefer to die here than be exiled in a land of heathens."

"What if we don't die at all?" The question rumbled from behind her.

Heart racing like a wild cony, she rounded on the eavesdropper and blew out a gale of a breath. "Telem!

I do not appreciate people listening to my private words."

"I did not listen. I heard." He shrugged, but his emotionless stare held the mystery of the man they first met in the cave. "Did I not warn you about the scouts? It seems your official's marriage arrangement has not kept us safe. Our neighbors from the east have joined Sanballat's armies from the north. They wait to plunder us."

Othniel fingered his blade. "How do you know the Ammonites are here? It is a sea of bodies beyond these rocks."

"I have only seen Sanballat," she added, not wanting Telem to think she was uniformed. "He rides his horse before his Samaritan army as if Nehemiah was his equal and not the cupbearer to the king."

Telem glanced off into the distance. "If Sanballat is laying siege then his ally Tobiah is holding his sword, for they are flies on the same corpse. And I will keep those traitors from stepping one foot into this city, or into the temple of our God." He punched a fist into his palm and with his tense stance Adah believed his threat. But how did Telem know of Tobiah, the governor of Ammon beyond the Jordan, for Telem's cave was on the wrong side of the river? Did more scouts come and hide in the hills?

"They are greedy." Othniel stood at her side, arms crossed, his hatred of their enemy rivaling Telem's. "Everyone in power fears losing the trade a rebirthed Jerusalem will take from their purse. They desire to win the king's favor by sending more taxes to the palace. Our landowners have no more to give."

Her friend's frustration was a firm vice upon her heart. He had labored for years during the drought to coax one more cluster of delicious grapes off the vine, or one more drip of olive oil into the jar. But rain had not come to aid his efforts.

"We will prevail." Her proclamation carried to the men crouched behind the rocks nearby. She had heard the conviction in Nehemiah's voice that night outside the city wall. His tears, his truth, drew her into his vision for the city, for it was God's vision. "The God of Abraham, Isaac, and Jacob will keep us safe."

Eyebrows raised, Telem cocked his head. "We are outnumbered?"

"What she spoke in the tunnel holds true." Othniel gave her a brief nod. Did he want her to repeat her challenge? "We must stand strong."

Surveying the faces around her, some bearded, some too young to grow hair, her chest swelled with pride like a strutting rooster. She believed her challenge that day while lying on the ground rejected by Telem, and she had to believe it this day. Had to believe. Had to speak out for justice.

She stepped away from Othniel toward men she did not know by name. "Be strong and courageous and God will act." Boldly, she repeated the phrase, picking up two rocks to add cadence to her plea.

Othniel echoed her charge. "Be strong and courageous and God will act."

David's wisdom to Solomon on finishing God's temple, grew louder, unfolding like a blanket along the wall. Swords clinked. Men stomped. The City of David would not be silent. Their cries and commotion spooked the mounts of their nearest enemies.

A horse neighed. She looked to the gate to see Nehemiah and the officials watching her bash two rocks together and sing out to her people. She stilled her beat and dropped the stones as a final reverberation quaked down her arms.

Nehemiah raised his right arm and urged his mount closer to the opposing governors. Sanballat of Samaria, and Tobiah of Ammon across the Jordan, moved their horses forward.

The chorus inside the wall quieted so discussions could be heard, but their defiant chant had gone forth like a messenger warning their foes of the people's determination to stand and do battle.

Soldiers rushed from the streets toward the gate and the nearby tower. Adah lost sight of her father as men fell in line in the rulers' wake. Turning to Othniel, and with a glance toward Telem, she said, "I want to keep watch on the officials. My father is in line to take the first arrows." She pointed to a large squared stone. "If you shift that brick, I can climb on it and peer over the heads of our men."

"Is that all I'm good for is moving rock?" Telem scoffed and held his position.

"Do you truly want an answer from her?" Othniel tipped the stone and rolled it end over end. His customary playful smirks had vanished.

"No." Telem grinned. "But I did manage to get you to do the work." He marched toward the fighting men defending the gate. Heads turned as Telem's tall, muscular frame stalked by.

She perched on the rock and with little effort was able to spy the traitorous leaders, Sanballat and Tobiah. Othniel set another stone in motion and joined her. He rested an arm on the arching jut of wall above their viewing area, and with his height he was a shield from the scorching sun. She turned to comment on Telem's rudeness, but staring into Othniel's ruddy face only a half-breath from hers, her witty words jumbled. Struck dumb, she licked her lips, but the moisture evaporated as did her rebuke of their mason.

"Don't worry." Othniel inspected the formation of the wall rising above her. "This stone is jagged. No sling stone can reach this spot."

"We'll be protected." Wasn't she always safe when Othniel was around? Turning toward the onslaught, she prayed. "Lord keep us safe."

Nehemiah opened his arms to the troops outside his city. "Why this show of force? Were my letters from Artaxerxes not enough for you? Or do you now serve another king?"

Sanballat acknowledged the strength of his armies with a sweep of his hand. His horse stepped forward as the reins went slack. Sanballat jerked his mount into submission. "You deceived us. Why rebuild this wall unless you plan to rise up against the king and overrun your neighbors?"

Adah pounded a fist on the wall. "We will protect ourselves like other cities," she muttered.

Swords raised into the air at her utterance.

"Why is Jerusalem any different than Samaria or Rabbath-Ammon?" Nehemiah held himself erect as if he was Artaxerxes in the flesh. His escorts from the king sat steadfast in their fine armor. "Shall my father's bones be trampled by travelers? The wall of this great city will stand as a testament to the faithfulness of our God." Nehemiah turned his attention to Tobiah. "Do you still call upon the name of *Adonai* in Ammon, or have you defiled yourself and your land for riches?"

Tobiah leaned back on his mount as if Nehemiah had reached over and slapped him. The squat leader scowled at the governor. "Of course, we serve the same

God. A daughter of Jerusalem births my grandchildren. We are of the same blood."

"Then go home." Adah's stiffened as neighbors turned her direction. Her comment carried farther than it ought.

Tobiah glanced in her direction. "Have I not been in the temple? The priests are known to me by name."

"As they are to me." Nehemiah boasted his relationship to all who could hear. "My plans are the same today as they were yesterday. Jerusalem will have a wall as strong as her people." Nehemiah's indigo robe draped down his arm as he held his hands toward the clouds.

"This is foolishness." Sanballat raised his silver-handled sword high into the air and struck at the wind. "You bring war upon your people because of a stubborn pride? Or is greed for trade riches making death acceptable in your eyes."

Tobiah cackled as if bloodshed held humor. His rust-colored robe jostled from his raucous scoff and the portly belly beneath. "A fox could topple your stone wall let alone the men of Ammon. But all is for naught. Our God has not seen fit to water your lands. You cannot even fill a barterer's basket."

"Do we serve the same God?" Nehemiah leaned on the horn of his saddle. "Killing a brother is in violation of the Law."

"We are not brothers," Tobiah shouted. He cast a glance at his ally, Sanballat. "You have made that clear, Nehemiah. Claiming this city as your own will bring judgment upon you. Heed my warning and repent of your selfishness."

Thrusting his arms out to the side, Nehemiah arched his back. "Throw your blade now. Let these witnesses see you kill the king's cupbearer. And who will you murder next? The king's own soldiers?"

Adah's heartbeat drummed a pulse through her ears. Her beloved Nehemiah waited, eyes closed, for his enemies to accept his challenge. How could he be certain of their restraint? Adah fingered and counted each sandalwood and chrysolite bead around her neck.

God of Abraham, spare your servant, Nehemiah.

Othniel stilled her methodic numbering. "God is with us. Not with our enemies." His breath breezed by her cheek.

She let her arm fall to her side. "I believe you speak the truth. God is with us."

Nehemiah dropped his arms and folded his hands in his lap, taking the reins of his mount in hand.

Sword half-raised, Sanballat trotted his horse forward until its nose almost touched the muzzle of Nehemiah's mount.

"You are not the king's only governor. This deception will not stand. Build if you dare." Sanballat strung out his admonition for everyone to hear. "Do not blame your fellow governors if these rocks crush your bones."

Sanballat sheathed his weapon and pranced his horse in front of his troops. He strutted north toward the main road to Samaria.

"Are dry bones worth the burying of new ones?" Tobiah fixed his narrow-eyed stare on Nehemiah. "Heed our wisdom and stop this offense."

The governor of Rabbath-Ammon retreated to the east with his band of men breaking ranks and roaming ahead of their leader's mount.

Praise be to God! Her father and Nehemiah were safe. "Can we trust their retreat?" she whispered to

Othniel.

"I do not believe this is just a warning. They could have sent a messenger for that." His hand rested upon her outer garment, near the lower part of her hip. His touch was not substantial enough for a public rebuke, but it let her know he prepared to fight for her lest their enemy turn and charge the wall. Othniel's gaze followed the path of Tobiah and his mounted men. "Why are some heading south away from their governors?"

Adah strained to see where the riders had gone. Tobiah's lands were to the east. Did his men seek a faster route through the fields? A tickle irritated her nose. She breathed deep, but her nostrils began to burn. Was someone heating pitch? She drew her veil over her cheeks and turned toward Othniel. Tears pooled in her eyes. "I need to get down."

Othniel bent low. "Are you ill?"

She shook her head and glanced beyond his shoulder over the rooftops of the city. Thin trails of white smoke rose above the distant rooftops. Her eyes flared.

"Speak, Adah. What is it?" Othniel asked.

Pointing to the east, she rasped, "Our fields are on fire. They've distracted us from protecting our lands."

11

Othniel leapt from his stone perch and disappeared into the crowd of battle-ready men. With her sight blurry from stinging tears, Adah was unable to navigate a descent fast enough to follow in her friend's path. *O' Lord do not let the fire be in Othniel's groves.* But even as she prayed protection on Othniel's ancestral land, her stomach hollowed. A wide haze of smoke billowed over what lay beyond the city wall. Hadn't the drought punished the farmers enough? Curse Sanballat and Tobiah for putting flame to groves of tinder.

She left her father in the care of Nehemiah and the king's cavalry and darted through the farmers shouting for aid. The chaos of cries in the streets sounded like wounded prey wailing in the night for comfort. How many more had to suffer?

A mumbled prayer escaped her lips as she raced toward a wall of black air, rising and overwhelming the wind. "Rescue us, O' Lord, from evil men." The remembrance of Sanballat's crooked-nose rebuke of Nehemiah sent her sandals slapping the ground faster and faster. "Protect us from men of violence." *Rescue Your people like You rescued our forefather David.* Hadn't the landowners suffered enough from rainless days?

Men jostled her near the Water Gate. Some carried large jars sloshing water into the dust. Others, hands on sheathed blades, followed the crumbling wall north.

No doubt in search of spies. The fresh planks of wood framing the gate and the resurrected stones abutting it, testified to the labors of her people. No wonder Sanballat and Tobiah were scared of a fortified Jerusalem.

After a few paces, she bent at the waist gasping to breathe. Heat and a shadowy haze taunted her lungs, daring her to continue into the outskirts of the city.

Around and around her face, she wrapped the length of her head covering so only her eyes peered past the cloth. Praise be that she knew the paths and terraced fields, for every tree limb and every laborer was shrouded in a ghostly fog.

Running north through lengths of raised beds, she slipped from her cloak and beat at the air as if it were her enemy. Tears streamed from her eyes of their own accord. Her lungs rebelled at her procession, burning with an ache that seeped into every rib. *I will not falter.*

As she neared Othniel's groves, her confidence became like the ash being swept away in the breeze, twisting every which way on its descent to the hardened soil below. Olive trees glowed like scarlet torches while their flames mingled with the blackest of smoke. Over the crackle of the boisterous fire she heard the whack of an ax. Male voices shouted warnings of falling trees. Her chest sunk to her belly as she viewed the devastation. Othniel had been faithful to assist her family and now he needed the debt repaid. And she would embrace her obligation.

In the terraced field below, a woman's wailing haunted Adah's soul. Through tear-filled eyes, she spied Othniel's mother and young brother battering grape vines with threadbare rugs. Flames devoured the shoots tied to parched wood. Adah raced down the main path to halt the fire's progress. She whipped her cloak at the fiery embers and joined in the attack.

"We need to break the trellis." Adah sputtered and coughed, trying to catch her breath. "Have an ax? Shovel?" Her mind devised words she could not speak.

Zipporah shook her head. "My husband—" She bent at the waist before slumping to the ground. Micaiah, her son, beat the sparks, defying their advance.

Kneeling near Zipporah, Adah inspected the woman's tunic for burns. "Are you hurt?"

"It is of no use." Zipporah wiped her cheeks. "The fire will not be smothered."

Adah scanned the vineyard. Her heart resounded a warning in her ears. Do something. Her mind spun, but her feet remained planted. Oh, where was a rock or tool when she had need of it?

Swirling ash stung her skin, but inside her belly an emboldened warmth blazed hotter than an ignited tree. Woe to the enemies of Judah. How dare they cause just people to suffer? She stalked toward Micaiah.

"Stand back." She charged the wooden planks on which the helpless plants stood impaled. Ramming her sandal into the trellis, she kicked with the force of a wild donkey. "Break," she demanded.

Cedar splintered under her barrage. On she went, attacking the length of wood, the length below, and the length above the stems of the plants. With every blow, energy burst forth from her body. She pointed to the next row at the edge of the field. "Micaiah. Break it. Let this drought be good for something."

The boy obeyed and smashed the trellis with renewed abandon.

Micaiah kicked. She kicked. She stopped to gather

the pieces of battered wood, piling them away from any flame. As she lifted the broken rods, her back stiffened, reminding her of her jarring assault. Her hands ached from the scrape of the trellis.

Zipporah came to Adah's side. The emboldened mother stomped on the bottom rung, breaking the defiant fire's path. She raised her arms high, turned, and swept Adah into a hug. "*Toda raba,* my daughter."

"*Slih'a,*" Adah muttered. "I am sorry our enemies targeted your land." How could she console Zipporah in the midst of so much loss?

Adah unwrapped herself from Zipporah's grief. Keeping the remaining vineyard safe was her foremost task. At least some of Othniel's lands would not see destruction. She glanced in the distance where a cut swath of land spared some olive trees from the advancing fire. Othniel, his brothers, and their wives had been successful in their labors. She closed her eyes and praised God. *Be strong and courageous and God will act.*

Landowners appeared from the smoky haze of distant fires and raced through an ash heap that was once a neighboring vineyard. "Riders," one shouted on his way to the city.

Mounts in Jerusalem were scarce. Adah picked up a stick and scanned the horizon. No Israelite would race through this commotion. Truly, not a friend of Jerusalem's governor.

Horse hooves drummed against the packed soil. A shiver cooled her heated skin. She reached for Zipporah. "We must return to the safety of our dwellings."

A stranger emerged from the east, sword raised, horse at a gallop. His weapon did not proclaim victory.

He meant to slay the enemy, and she was what he sought. His stare bore into her like a well-aimed spear. *I am his enemy.*

Shoving Zipporah to the ground, Adah reached for a splintered trellis. Micaiah, still as a sculpted idol, held his ground. "Get your brothers," she yelled. Her mouth tasted like sour goat's milk. The boy did not move. "Now!"

Adah gripped the wood. Her hand sizzled with the slice of sharp bark. She would tend the splinters later if God spared her from this warrior, for now she would fight the pagan who intended to strike down the daughter of a ruler, a daughter of Jerusalem. She focused on the intruder's wild-eyed stare, and hurled the broken trellis at his face. The thrust of her arm caused it to ache as if it had dislodged from her shoulder.

End over end, her trellis sailed toward the horse and rider. Balking at the incoming object, the rider's mount spooked. Every muscle bulged on the grand animal as it sidestepped and turned to retreat. The wooden rod struck the rider in the chest. Falling, it grazed the belly of his mount. Back and forth, the horse's head jerked, tugging on the reins, and urging its rider to set it free. The raider cursed.

Adah launched another plank of wood.

With all the lurching and panic of his horse, her enemy did not duck, and the solid rod did not miss. *Crunck.* Trellis struck temple. The raider's head snapped backward. He slumped to the side and off his saddle. His mount bucked to be gone. The warrior's weapon slipped from his hand and crashed to the dirt between her and its owner. Her foe smacked the ground hard and began scurrying out of the path of his horse's hooves. He rushed toward his blade.

Rage simmered inside of Adah. How dare this foreigner threaten her life and the lives of her friends? Head throbbing as if it would burst, she unsheathed the knife in her belt and lunged to obtain the sword. Woe to the raider if he retrieved his weapon before she did, as she was ready to sink her small blade into his flesh. No enemy of Judah would claim victory this day.

A short distance from his weapon, the rider froze. Eyes as wide as plums, he stepped away from his possession, and sprinted to his horse. He leapt onto his mount while shouts berated his retreat.

She turned to see Othniel and his brothers racing toward her. Blowing out a breath, she let her shoulders slump to her breast. *Selah!*

Othniel marched her direction, brows furrowed, with lips ribbon-thin. "Can't you stay inside the city?" His voice was loud enough to draw another attacker. Hands on hips, he halted too close to her. "You could have been slaughtered." His family gawked at his outburst.

Heat sprawled from her neck into her cheeks. How dare he berate her after she saved his mother and his vineyard? "I can protect myself." She held up her blade.

"With that?" He pointed at her knife. "One lunge from that pagan and you would have been killed."

"God gave me the victory. That coward ran from my wrath." She sheathed her weapon. "I came to help your family save some of their lands, and save some I did."

"We can save our own land." Othniel slapped the side of his ax into his palm. "You have no stake in these fields."

A lash would have hurt less. Hadn't she and her mother scouted these lands with Othniel for years? What of her efforts to keep Zipporah from being beheaded? Her face blazed from his reprimand. His family gathered a few feet away, dumbstruck.

"We all have a stake in these lands," she shouted.

A few of Othniel's brothers nodded their agreement, but no one berated their brother.

Othniel brushed a soot-black hand through his ash-covered hair. He shook his head as if her answer held no merit. "Come, I will escort you back inside the city. I want to make sure no harm befalls you."

"No." Her response came out too harsh for her liking. She turned her back on her friend and picked up the fallen sword, grasping it with two hands to keep it from wobbling and betraying her crushed spirit. "It is not necessary. Your father may have need of you." She held up the long blade. "With this, I do not require an escort. I am my own guard."

Whirling around, she traipsed toward the city with her hand throbbing and her dignity shattered like a trellis.

12

Adah shuffled through the streets of Jerusalem, hiding the raider's sword in her outer garment and ignoring the glances of passersby. With her veil still wrapped around her face, and a scorched hem and tattered cloak, she resembled a desert traveler. A haze of smoke hovered above the city's rooftops. A testament to the hatred of Sanballat and Tobiah.

Forcing an all-is-well smile onto her face, she entered her home. Her mother sat in the living area, alone, with a mortar balanced in her lap and a basket of wheat kernels nearby. A sash the color of muted rose petals hung across the crisp folds of her robe. Fortunately for Adah, her mother could not behold the soot-stained rags from the grove.

"*Shalom,* mother." Adah bent and kissed her mother's forehead. "Where's Judith?"

Elisheba set the pestle in the mortar. "Your sister is taking a meal to your father. But you my child were not near a simple cooking fire, for the scent of smoke has filled this room."

Adah tensed. Should she confess about the peril? No rebuke could rival Othniel's. "Zipporah's fields were set ablaze by a band of Samaritans. I went to beat at the flames."

"With Othniel?" Her mother's question rang out as a statement.

Why did her mother always assume she was with

Othniel? "After Othniel. He fled from the wall so fast I could not keep up with him."

Her mother gestured for Adah to sit near her chair. "Did God grant us favor? I have been offering prayers for our fighting men." Hope and hesitation rang in her mother's words.

"Some favor." Adah unwrapped the veil from her head and rested at her mother's side. She balanced on a pillow embroidered with scarlet, indigo, and purple threads. Her mother's elaborate handiwork was but a memory now. "The governors did not attack Nehemiah and our men at the gate, but their scouts started fires in the fields. Half of Othniel's main grove is gone. We saved most of the vineyard. Some plants are damaged. I pray they will recover."

"I'm sure Zipporah and Othniel are grateful for your labors."

Othniel's rebuke echoed in Adah's mind. "I believe so."

"I know so." Her mother stroked Adah's veil and stretched out a few tight curls freed by the burnt linen. "You have a compassionate spirit."

"Do I?" Tears pulsed behind Adah's eyes. She would not let them out and trouble her mother. "Since your illness, I have been trying to learn how to spice the myrrh for the temple. I've had to travel farther in search of useful scents. Now, with a wall to build, I am scarcely home to attend to your needs."

"Foolishness." Cupping Adah's chin, her mother lifted her daughter's face so their eyes almost met. Adah adjusted her gaze. "You have taken over my duties without a complaint and worked in the heat to honor your father's name. Because of you, his name will be recorded for future generations. And if I had to guess, you were too close to the flames sparing the lands around the city."

I've learned mercy from you. Adah gripped the carved oak armrest of her mother's chair. Elisheba, wife of Shallum, was more just and upright than any queen in Susa. "I couldn't stand idle and let the fields burn."

Her mother caressed Adah's cheek and then fumbled for her waiting pestle. "I know you want to be there for everyone, but it is impossible. Your heart beats for too many people. And some circumstances are beyond our control. We must wait on God to act."

"Where is God?" Adah poked at a frayed indigo thread on the pillow and smoothed a finger over the pattern. "Why does He withhold the rain from our crops? Couldn't He have stopped Sanballat's schemes?"

"He sent us Nehemiah." Dropping a few more kernels into the mortar, her mother felt for the height of her flour. "Our God will never turn His face from us. We must be patient."

"But while we wait, others struggle to eat. We are not in debt. We have provisions for our table. Taxes do not burden us." Adah wrapped her arms around her knees and inhaled the aroma of a campfire. "Why call Nehemiah into service and allow Sanballat and Tobiah to threaten the city? Am I wrong to seek an answer from God for all this turmoil?"

"You may ask, humbly. You may not demand." Muscles tensed on her mother's arm as she ground the wheat. "Answers do not always come. Not in our time."

Adah's chest ached with every breath. Was it from the fires, or watching a simple task become a chore for the blind? "I never received an answer about your sight."

"Oh, Daughter." Elisheba placed her stone instruments on the floor and held out her hands for Adah to take hold. "How long did I pray for a child? When I thought my time had passed, God blessed me with two babies. Our people wandered in the desert for forty years. Did they not ask when it would end? Build the wall one stone upon another. God will finish it in His time. His way."

"My tasks would be easier if I were a man." Adah sighed. She doubted Othniel would have berated her if she were six feet tall and muscled like a laborer. He shouldn't have raised his voice at all. Did he expect her to do nothing after all the years of friendship they had shared? He knew her too well to watch her sit idle.

Her mother squeezed Adah's hands and held tight. "My tasks would not be easier if I had birthed an heir. If I had a son, he would be with his father, and not at home. You and Judith bring me joy each and every day. You make me proud, and I know your father feels the same. Who else can boast of a daughter raising the city wall?"

"Could we pray that one other family has a daughter join their labors?" Adah laughed and kissed her mother's hands before releasing them. "Perhaps then we would not be the only family discussed over meals." Slowly she stood and tested her tired legs. "Judith and I may have to work longer days on the wall. I don't know if Othniel will return to help us. His lands are in need of attention."

"Oh." Her mother's short answer was drawn out and filled with understanding "Then it is a good thing the Lord saw fit to remind me of Telem. We have his service. You do not need to rely so much on Othniel"

"I know. I am glad Telem saw fit to help us." Adah expected admonishment from her gruff mason. Not from her friend. "It is still not the same."

"Then your sister and I will do more. Whatever we can." Her mother sat straighter and leaned forward as if waiting for instructions. "Even though I cannot see, I am here for you. God has not taken my strength. I am able to do His bidding. I can blend more mortar."

"You can do whatever you want. I am confident in that." Adah laughed with a renewed spirit. Her mother's brown eyes sparkled as if sitting in darkness was not a hardship, but a blessing. A knot of emotion tightened against Adah's ribs. *I will not let my family down.*

Pressing a kiss to her mother's temple, she said, "God has provided what we have needed so far. He will not abandon His people." She strolled to where her newly won sword lay basking in the window's light. "Although, if we are building this wall forty years from now, I may question God anew."

13

Even after washing the soot from her skin and soaping her scalp, Adah's hair still smelled like smoke. Pulling a ringlet taut to her nose, she breathed in fire-tainted cassia and lye. Perhaps laboring in the night air would calm her anger over Sanballat's tricks. Displaying her newly won sword, she cinched a belt around her tunic and winced. One fairly good-sized splinter had pierced her skin with a vengeance. War had come to Jerusalem's gates, and a small gash would not keep her from fighting for her city—a city in desperate need of a fortified wall.

She scraped her fingernail over the thin scrap of wood embedded in her palm and hooked enough of an end to pinch and yank it from her flesh. Victory had been hers this day and soon her people would be free from the daily threat of their enemies. She didn't need Othniel or his brothers to protect her beyond the city wall. God had rewarded her bravery with a fine sword.

Behind the distant mountains, the sun dipped, abandoning the city to a night of unknown threats. She hurried toward her father's assigned place on the wall. They would need to build faster with enemies lurking in the outskirts of the city. Would more fires be set in the cover of darkness, or did the Samaritans wish to draw blood in the shadows?

Rounding the pile of rubble from the crumbling corner of the vacant house, she breathed in the aroma of boiling sap, Telem's secret rock coating. She shortened her steps. Her stone mason certainly did not slumber. He was surrounded by Nehemiah, Ezra the priest, Rephaiah, and her father. Othniel was nowhere in sight. Her friend could shout at his brothers all he wanted while clearing debris from his fields.

Rephaiah glanced her direction. What was the ruler of another district doing on this side of the city? Why wasn't he with his cherished sons building their assigned section?

Her sword lay heavy on her hip. She shifted it toward her back and joined the small band of men, giving a slight bow in a show of respect to her elders. "You are safe, Governor. I feared for you and my father and for everyone who ventured outside the gate."

Nehemiah's head bobbed. He reached out a hand as if to withdraw her sword from its borrowed sheath.

Pivoting, she stepped back and clasped a hand to the hilt of her sword.

"It appears I am not the only one who left the confines of the city." The governor's cocked head and raised eyebrows suggested a rebuke, but his eyes flashed with a familiarity she saw the night he wept in her presence.

"I went to fight the fires." Her mind scrambled for more words. Under the perusal of her father, she tried to swallow and choked. "I beat at the flames to save our fields." Her voice cracked as if she still breathed scorched air. Her gaze fell on every man in the huddle. "A raider lost his sword when his horse spooked. He prized his horse more than his weapon. So now his blade will keep us safe."

"That soldier may return." Nehemiah glanced at

an opening in the piled rock. "For now the city is quiet, but we will need guards along the wall. Where rubble is strewn about, keen eyes must keep watch."

"We are spread far apart," Ezra added. His priestly robe flowed as he indicated the distance between the workers. "At the first sign of trouble, the priests are ready to sound the trumpet. Our temple servants will watch and pray."

Her father nodded. "We will not be caught unaware. Work will continue through the night."

"Every night?" she asked.

"Stars or no stars." Telem straightened as if she had uttered an offense.

Ezra folded his hands and splayed some tassels on his priestly robe. "You are fortunate to have Telem's skills. His father helped rebuild our temple." He nodded toward Telem. "I am glad you have returned."

Telem seemed to grow taller with the priest's praise. "If only my father would have lived to see the wall rebuilt."

"Why are you not working with the priests?" Rephaiah looked to Ezra. The elder priest shrugged, but gave no explanation.

Was Telem from a priestly line? Why was a Levite living in a cave?

"Why didn't you hire more priests to do the work," Rephaiah asked her father. "Your daughters cannot be of much use."

Heat flamed up Adah's neck and into her cheeks. How dare Rephaiah insult her family in the presence of the governor? Her father may not have an heir, but he had a daughter who would protect this city with her life. Man or no man. Othniel or no Othniel.

"I was sought by Shallum's daughters," Telem

interjected. "To assist my city."

Rephaiah glowered at her as if she were a harlot. "You went into the outskirts to seek a man?"

Her head jerked backward at his scorn. "With an escort, of course."

"At my wife's behest." Her father's voice grew too loud for the intimate huddle near the pitch pot. "Our lands are known to my daughter since she traveled with Elisheba."

"My daughter tends to her husband's needs." Rephaiah cast his chastisement around the circle. "Perhaps it is time you sought the same position for your daughters. Surely Shallum, one of your servants could see to your wife's welfare."

"My mother's perfumes have been sought by the rulers of Egypt." Adah's rebuttal shot out like an arrow aiming for Rephaiah's puffed chest. "She is not a burden to me or my sister."

"Obviously." Rephaiah clicked his tongue for emphasis. "For your days are spent laboring among the men."

"To do the work of God." Her voice quaked, her hands trembled, even her hem shook, but she would not stay silent.

Nehemiah clapped his hand upon her father's shoulder. "I have seen your wife laboring in the sun. Her work is a testimony to her faith in God." The governor stepped over a freshly cut stone. "We must be on our way to carry our message of warning to the people. Walk with us, Shallum. You can make introductions."

"Gladly." Her father cast a glance at her sword and frowned. "Carry on. The wall is making great progress." His praise rang hollow, for Adah was quite certain she saw a slight shake of his head.

Did her father regret their vow at the assembly? A gusty trade wind pimpled her flesh. She rubbed her arm with her uninjured hand and remembered her pledge. She had no regrets for honoring her family and defending her home. Not this night. Not ever.

"Rephaiah." Ezra ambled over to the stiff-necked ruler. "Let us inspect the work of the temple servants on the Fish Gate." The revered priest practically swept Rephaiah in the direction of the temple and his Levite laborers.

When the guests had left, Telem blew out a harsh breath. The grunt startled Adah, bringing her thoughts around to the goal set before her, and not upon her father's concern.

"I am sorry I raised Rephaiah's ire." Telem stooped to pick up a cutting blade.

"You?" Adah scoffed. "I raise his ill regard better than anyone."

"Because your faith in God challenges his own." Telem knelt by an oblong rock.

"I don't see how? His family is also following Nehemiah's call to build the wall. With many sons, the work is being done faster." She shifted her sword so it was in full view.

"But what does it cost him to have his sons do the work?" Telem pounded the stone like a warning drum and then exchanged his blade for a chisel. "Where are the calluses on his hands?"

On mine. She glanced at her battered hands.

"Jehu. Jehuliel," Telem shouted for the brothers, interrupting their labors. "Strap on your weapons and guard the rubble."

For a moment, the brothers stood idle as they

contemplated the sizeable rock. Adah's countenance sunk. How would she have the strength for such a task?

With Telem's order for the brothers to be sentries, that would mean only two able-bodied men—Telem and Othniel—would work with her and Judith to construct the wall. And that was if Othniel returned from clearing his ravaged fields. The height of her father's wall would suffer. If they lagged behind the other sections, more guards would be needed to defend the area.

She fingered the hilt of her blade. "I will stand watch. All I need is a man's cloak. No scout will suspect a woman wields such a sword."

Her fellow workers stood rooted to the ground.

Raising her weapon, she shouted, "A sword for the Lord!"

A servant bringing water placed the vessel near the fire and scampered off without a word.

Turning his back to her, Telem lumbered toward the brothers. He flapped his hand to send them to their posts.

She charged after her mason. If she were an ox, she would have trampled him, hoof to his back. "Why do you ignore my offer? Allow me to stand guard. Did I not scour your cave? You praised my efforts to a ruler of Jerusalem." She rounded on Telem. "Other workers are not far away. Will I not be within a shout? I know this area better than a man gone for years." Not desiring to insult the brothers, she said, "Or men newly arrived." She pointed at a squared boulder. "I cannot wedge such a rock on my own."

"It is the truth." Jehu regarded her and then glanced at the sizeable stone.

"We are men of Judah." Jehuliel came to his brother's aid. "Are we not feared for our skill as fighters? No army would believe a woman stands as one of our soldiers."

Her posture softened. She was not alone in this argument. A rush of energy surged through her body as she beheld her new allies questioning Telem's command.

"This is madness." Telem kicked at his cutting block. "The law forbids a woman dressing as a man."

"Nonsense." Her hands fisted into tight knots. "All I need is an oversized cloak. My clothing will not change. I am dressed as a woman."

Jehu edged closer. "The daughter of Shallum speaks the truth. We all know she is not a man."

"Jehu!" Telem snapped. "You care to uphold this foolish plan?"

Judith strode into the work area, mixing a bowl of gums for Telem's pitch pot. "It appears I am the only one still working."

Telem huffed. "Talk some sense into your sister. She intends to stand guard this night."

Her twin sister set her mixture down and slapped her hands. "Not without me, she doesn't. Sentries go forth in pairs"

Pacing like a caged beast, their mason scanned the length of the wall. "Where is your father?"

"Will their mother do?" Elisheba neared with the assistance of a walking stick and an elderly neighbor.

"Yes." Telem stomped toward their mother. "Your daughters are insisting to stand guard through the night." Telem's voice was but a low rumble.

Smiling, her mother swept her arm as if to introduce herself. "Better my daughters than me."

Adah laughed and then sobered.

Telem snatched a sharpened blade lying near his tools and handed it to Judith. "At least be well armed like your sister."

Judith beamed. Jehu handed Adah his cloak and ducked away from Telem's reach.

Adah fingered the hilt of her blade. "May God strike down any invaders this night. And if He doesn't, I will."

14

Blinking into the star-lit shadows, Adah scanned the surrounding rocks and bushes for movement. Would Sanballat and Tobiah attack after burning the fields? Surely, they knew Nehemiah would not change course when he believed God had called him to the city for this purpose. She would not change course either, for she desired to see her city restored to its greatness.

Adah strolled a short distance to the south where most of the wall had been torn down by Babylonian soldiers many years ago. With a two-brick-high foundation, this section of the wall could be easily breeched. Leaning against a single formation of shoulder-high rock, she could barely make out the form of her sister plodding north.

Spread out campfires inside the city sent an eerie glow into the night as if the wall itself was the guardian between light and darkness. She did her job and methodically watched the wilderness for any sign of peril. Hebrew chatter and stone scraping made hearing an intruder's advance difficult. Occasionally, she ambled closer to the next group of workers. Their sentry gave her a nod. If only he knew she wasn't Jehu.

After hours of pacing, her feet ached at the slightest scuff of her sandals. She stationed herself against the lonely tower of stones and lifted a knee to rest her throbbing toes.

Someone leapt over the ruins.

She gasped. Her hand whipped to her sword. Still as a stone, she waited to see if the person was Hebrew or half-breed. Wild drumming in her ears drowned out the clinks and thumps of the distant masons. A well-placed lunge of an enemy sword and these tall stones would mark her corpse. Licking her lips, she prepared to growl out a warning and then fight for her life.

"Adah?" The summons was too friendly to be a foe.

Her chest practically sunk to her knees as she blew out a pent up breath. "Othniel?" she whispered. "I could have called men down on you." Would he have blamed her for that confrontation too?

He closed the gap between them. "A spy wouldn't know your name." He spoke as if they sauntered to find another root or bud for her oils. "And he wouldn't call out to a woman."

Surveying any tree or trench in the vicinity, she kept her gaze from his face. Why did he have to always make sense? "So, you have spoken to Telem." She peered over her shoulder. Friend, or not, Othniel was a distraction from her duty. And he had not made amends for humiliating her in front of his family. "Does he know you are here?"

She stepped around her visitor and headed farther south. Being trapped between rocks and Othniel's chest made her belly rise and plummet like an ocean's wave.

"Yes, he does." He fell in beside her, matching her footfalls.

Silence reigned, but she could smell the jasmine and sage his mother Zipporah must have mixed in with her lye to wrest the soot from his tunic. The aroma of Othniel in the starlight made her forget some of the injustice she had suffered earlier.

Their lack of words haunted her. She searched for a topic to banter about and settled on their mystery mason.

"Our Telem is the son of a priest. You were not here when Ezra praised Telem's father for helping rebuild the temple."

Othniel slowed his steps. "Then why was he in a cave and not helping with temple duties?"

She shrugged. "That is something to ponder for I do not know of any wife who desires to live in a rock?"

"Perhaps she never did?" Othniel breathed deep and stopped walking altogether. "I smell clove oil." His gaze rested on her bandage. "You're hurt."

She pressed her lips together and stifled a grin. He had deciphered the scent of her healing oil. Her mother had taught their escort well. Keeping her stare fixed on a sprawling acacia tree, she flexed her hand. A stinging burn shot up her arm and ignited a tingling sensation behind her eyes. She crinkled her nose and adjusted her grip on her sword. "It's a tiny cut."

"I knew you were wounded in the uproar." His tone praised his miraculous knowledge while chastising her courage.

"I was hurt by a trellis." *And by you.* "Not by the raider." She edged farther from the wall and into the darker shadows, far enough from the laborers so they wouldn't notice her companion.

He followed and bent low to invade the privacy her cloak gave to her face. "My mother said you threw a rod at that heathen."

Warmth prickled from her neck into her cheeks. This was her Othniel. Excited about her victory. A woman's victory. "Everything happened so fast. I did what I could to stay alive. But I did not tell my mother or my family that I faced a rider."

"Why not? You saved half my vineyard."

His acknowledgement filled her with enough energy to race around the city, but remembering the enemy's snarled mouth and bloodthirsty eyes sent a chill through her veins. She shivered even though she was covered by a mound of cloth. "I don't like to ponder what would have happened if you and your brothers had not arrived."

"You would have run to safety." He sounded like he truly believed in her well-being.

She shook her head. "I'm not as sure as you. His sword was within my reach."

"Is that why you are out here? For revenge?"

"I don't want to take a life." Her cheeks flamed. How could she make him understand her intentions? "I believe building this wall means something to Nehemiah, and it means something for our people. I cannot lift as much as a man can, but I want to do my part. Small as it may be."

Othniel brushed a hand through his dark hair. "I wish I had your faith that helping Nehemiah would lift the hardship from our people and end the drought and strife." Even under a black sky, his eyes caught the starlight and brightened as though tiny torches flamed inside each brown orb. The embers from his eyes warmed her soul. "I will assist you, Adah, as much as I can for as long as I can."

Her belly fluttered as if someone had released a pent up dove.

He stepped closer. Too close. But then who would notice? "I should never have doubted you in the vineyard." His hand caressed the top of hers, but he did not inspect her wound. "We sang about strength and courage, and when you faced..." his words swept into the night. He lifted her hand, all the while stroking her skin with the softest touch she'd ever experienced. "Please forgive me."

Acceptance caught in her throat. She threw back her shoulders and stood a little straighter, trying to look more girl than guard. The sensations created by the stroke of his hand ricocheted from her arm to her toes. "There were times I believed God had forgotten us. But I don't believe that now." She met his piercing gaze. "I forgive you, Othniel."

His face lit up as though he had found a pouch of gold coins. "*Toda raba.*" He stepped backward, but his hand stayed wrapped around hers. "I'd better return before Telem notices I have been gone too long for one drink. Stay alert this night, my brave Adah."

Her feet begged to follow him back inside the city, but she stood her post. "I will."

Hesitating, he closed the gap between them and branded her temple with a kiss.

She would have sworn legions of armies shook the ground beneath her feet. Mouth gaping, she was unable to fumble a response.

Without another word, Othniel turned, ran, and then leapt over a low section of the wall.

Her pulse pounded a deafening rhythm between her ears. A raider could have galloped a horse straight toward her and she would have been none the wiser.

She whirled and beheld the outskirts, scanning the closest bushes, boulders, and trees. One thing was for certain. On this night, she gave the illusion of being a man, a fierce guard of the city, but inside her body, from her feet rooted to the ground to the tips of her curls touching the hood of Jehu's cloak, a sensation awakened—an inner-knowledge that whether guarding, fighting, or building, she wanted Othniel at her side.

15

Three days passed.

Sanballat and his army of Samaritans stayed north in their own lands. Tobiah and his Ammonite followers did not show their treasonous faces. Had Nehemiah convinced the governors that his intentions were to rebuild the city of his fathers and not wage a blood battle or trade war? Or did fear of retribution from King Artaxerxes shackle their greedy hearts?

Telem, Othniel, and the brothers stacked stone upon stone, laboring vigorously and more hours than she cared to count. Her father relieved the men one by one, so they could rest and progress on their section of the wall continued uninterrupted. If every family worked as hard as hers, Nehemiah's vision for Jerusalem would come to pass very soon.

With the sun not yet risen, she and Judith hurried to take a brief nap—the darkness still a shroud to their identity.

The light revealed who truly guarded Shallum's area: his daughters.

Adah stepped through an opening in the wall near the next party of workers. Hanun and his kin were rebuilding the Valley Gate and the walls around the wooden frame. Her father's section was already more than waist high and too much of a climb in a dress. A burst of pride buoyed her weary bones at the progress her friends had made.

In the distance, Othniel and Jehu layered cut stones. As she neared their campfire, Othniel glanced her direction. The flicker of firelight revealed sunken half-moons under his eyes. Dark bristles of a beard shadowed his jaw. When had he last slept? With all the urgency of building the wall, they had barely spoken of his kiss. Perhaps he only thought it an apology. Her stomach cinched. She did not need another apology, but she desired another kiss.

Hurrying toward the water jars, she filled cups, and sipped some refreshment for herself. She carried drinks to Othniel and Jehu, and ignored remarks about thirst from Telem and Jehuliel. She shook her head. Why was it men liked to be served? She would see to them in a moment.

"When can you rest?" She handed a drink to Othniel. His breaths came out in short pants after heaving a rock into place.

He tipped his head back as if to soak in the last of the starlight. "We need to secure another level." The sling of his garment underneath his arm revealed an indentation of ribs.

Did Zipporah have enough coin saved to feed her sons and daughters-in-law? She squeezed the cup in her hand, grateful it would not shatter. "When did you last eat?"

He chugged the water she offered. "You may have enough vigor to ask, but I am too tired to answer."

"Then I will spur my mother and the servants on to bring us some stew and bread. I may even bake the bread myself."

"That would be an accomplishment grander than this wall." He smiled briefly, but somehow his eyes stayed somber as if the weight of the rocks had crushed his spirit.

"Wait and see." She took the cup from him. "You will find I am a guard with hidden talents."

"I already know how talented you are." A slight grin erased the weariness from his face.

Was he referring to their kiss? Her belly fluttered. Couldn't be. He meant her perfumes. "I have help finding the freshest buds." She avoided his gaze. "*Toda raba.*"

He leaned in, his eyes finally meeting hers. "I meant you are the only woman building this wall, save your sister. And whatever scented oils you have put together are making our labor in the sun bearable. Your mother would be proud." His eyes glimmered. "I am not bold enough to speak of other talents."

Her eyes widened. "You shall not," she whispered.

"Never." Growing serious, he stepped away. "Remember what I have said."

Blossoms sprouted from her heart. She wanted to sing, *come back, come back, don't stray very far, your bread will be in the oven.* Her head was in the stars. But this was not the time to discuss their kiss, or its intentions, for too many men lingered nearby. They had plenty of time to talk later. "Don't I always heed your wisdom?" *Save, maybe once.*

Othniel hesitated before dipping his trowel into the mortar. "Bring me that meal." His dark-eyed focus on her was like a welcome caress.

"I will bring the best." Well, the best she could make. And the sooner she returned home, the sooner her laborers would eat. She remembered Telem and Jehuliel, offering them water before racing around the crumbling corner and down an alley toward home.

Little more than an hour later, Adah carried bread

to the worksite. The warmth of the loaf seeped through the linen, and into her hands. Stew would be served later, but she managed to add a few raisin cakes from her father's provisions to the basket she carried. With the dew of the morning snatched away, all she heard was the *scritch* of Telem's cutting blade, a sound that had grown as soothing to her as a gracefully strummed harp.

She searched for Othniel. He was not in sight.

"Where is Othniel?" she asked her master mason.

Telem halted his shaping. His eyes grew wide as melons as he beheld her basket. He bent forward and sniffed the air. "Surely, that is not all for the boy." He called for Jehu and Jehuliel to join him.

"Of course you may have some, but I promised Othniel I would bring bread." On tip-toe, she peeked over Telem's shoulder for her friend.

"You made this?" Telem's eyebrows arched as he lifted the cloth.

"Judith helped."

The brothers charged her. "I do not care who made it. I would sneak it from the enemy." Jehu lined up behind Telem.

The men jostled her arm as they helped themselves to her bread.

Adah glanced beyond the wall. "Did he take the mule to fetch another rock?"

"Who?" Telem chewed furiously.

"Othniel," she huffed. Give a man some food to fill his belly and his mind empties.

Telem shrugged. "I have not seen him for a while. Maybe he sleeps."

She offered the first raisin cake to Jehu since his cloak was her disguise, but her worry centered on

Othniel. "We talked earlier and he did not mention taking a break."

"I saw him head east shortly after you left." Jehu bit into a sweet cake and swallowed hard. "I thought you sent him on an errand."

"He lives that direction." She secured the remaining food. "I will bring his meal to his house." Giddiness drained from her body. During her baking, she'd envisioned her friend's face alive with surprise. "Maybe his mother needs him to help barter in the markets this morning."

"Tell the boy to hurry back. We have not seen the last of our enemies. A higher wall will give us cover." Telem patted his stomach and smacked his lips. "Tell your sister I am thankful for her food."

"Not mine?" She smirked at her mason and gave the pitch pot a one-armed stir. "I will be back soon."

Telem held up a bucket of limestone. "I hope with the boy."

She hoped so too. She turned and headed toward Othniel's house.

Avoiding scaffolding, strewn tools, and laborers toiling on the wall, she headed north, and up a hill before crossing the straight street to the Horse Gate. She scanned the merchant booths but didn't see Othniel or his mother. Oh, how she wanted Othniel to taste her bread. He could eat his fill for his faithfulness. He had paid for the price of her pearled perfume jar tenfold. All without a complaint. He rarely returned home, preferring to sleep with Telem and the brothers near the fire and washing vessels.

As she neared Zipporah's house, a haunting wail, long and grief-stricken erupted from the home. With a hand over her basket, Adah sprinted toward the door.

Did Othniel hurt himself this morning? Is that why he'd left his labors? Surely no raiders had returned to the fields. If they had, the city would be in an uproar.

Without a single knock, she burst through the door. No mat or woven rug stopped her slide. The inside of Othniel's home felt as withered as his grape vines.

Zipporah sat slumped on the floor, two daughters-in-law at her side. The women smoothed their mother-in-law's hair and wiped her tears with their veils. Othniel's younger brother, Micaiah, huddled in the corner, hands over his ears.

Adah flung her basket on the dining table and knelt before Zipporah. The mother had not been this distraught facing a sword-wielding enemy.

"What has happened? Tell me your troubles." Adah clasped one of Zipporah's hands between her own. Only a throb from her injury greeted her compassion.

Tears streamed down the older woman's cheeks. "My son is gone."

A chill swept over Adah's skin. Oh, Lord, not Othniel. She wouldn't entertain such a thought. Zipporah had many sons. Many who worked far out in the fields. "Who is gone?"

Zipporah's chest heaved. She sniffled and tried to cover her face with her free hand. No name came forth.

"My brother, Othniel." The weak and hesitant reply came from the corner.

Adah released Zipporah's hand and whipped around, settling onto the floor while balancing her weight with one hand. Micaiah rocked forward, his arms wrapped tight around his knees. Unspent tears glistened in his eyes. "My brother is gone and he isn't coming home."

She flinched. It wasn't true. Her arms trembled as she tried to brace herself from falling flat onto the barren floor. She had seen Othniel a few hours ago. How could he be gone without a single word, a single goodbye, a single kiss? Othniel had been with her since the beginning, believing she could fulfill her vow when others mocked her labors. She wouldn't let him slip away without sharing her gratitude and her love. They had begun this project together, and they would finish it side by side.

Adah rounded on Zipporah. "Where has he gone?"

Zipporah's chest shuddered with pent up grief. "My Othniel," she sobbed.

He's my Othniel.

In her most official sounding voice, Adah commanded, "Tell me now."

16

"I tried, Adah. Truly, I tried to keep my son." Zipporah rocked back and forth. Her daughters-in-law did little to still her movements. "Without the rain, there were no grapes to make into wine and no olives to press into oil. What can I sell? My storeroom is empty of wares."

Adah perched on her knees, willing Zipporah to answer her question. "Where is he now?" Faster and faster her heart raced. She desired to know more, needed to know more. With every delay, Othniel traveled farther from the city.

The tearful mother reached out and grasped Adah's hands. "We had no more money to give. My husband waited as long as he could."

"For what?" Pressure in Adah's chest felt as though it would burst her lungs.

"Othniel is to labor so we have silver to pay our taxes." Zipporah's fervent grip pained Adah's injured palm. "We have to keep our land."

"The deal has been struck," a daughter-in-law confirmed.

"No!" Adah's denial came out harsh as a lash. She drew back. Othniel was gone to settle a debt? "This cannot be. He is building with my family. Here in Jerusalem." Her gaze swiveled from mother to daughters-in-law, but their expressions remained steadfast. "I must go to him. Tell me where he is."

"He is gone. He cannot return." Zipporah's countenance sobered. Her marketplace prowess overshadowed her mourning. "My husband arranged for an early payment so Rephaiah cannot threaten our lands. Our taxes are paid for the time being."

Would Zipporah sell another son? There had to be a better way. Nehemiah came to rebuild the city and call her people home. Not send them away. Reasoning raced through Adah's mind. "Your son escorted my mother and I all over these lands. Why didn't you seek out me or my father?"

"Who has your father helped?" Zipporah's face wrinkled with accusation. "Has Shallum forgiven payments?"

Heat flashed from Adah's chest into her cheeks. "My father is a righteous man."

Zipporah wiggled free from her daughters-in-law. "So is my husband. We have the same number of sons and daughters to feed with half our land and a meager harvest. The officials are not blind to our struggles, but their hearts are as hard as the soil."

"May it not be so?" Adah's knees became like chaff. She had witnessed the distress of the landowners, but only God could send rain—not an official. "This drought has caused many good people to suffer."

"Some more than others." Whether she meant them to or not, Zipporah's words cast judgment.

Adah's temples throbbed. Had her own mother's blindness distracted her family? When she met Zipporah's stare, Adah's heart pinched. "Please forgive me if I have caused you pain. But tell me where your son has gone, for I did not say my *Shalom* and I have brought him food I had promised for his labors. May he not go hungry again."

Shaking her head, Zipporah pressed her lips together. "You are an official's daughter. I will not be responsible for sending you out of the city after the encounter we had with the rider."

"I am going with or without your assistance." She did not turn her face from Zipporah but inwardly willed the mother's heart to soften. "Do not make me search in vain. For I will not stop until I find him."

"Girl, there is nothing you can do." Tears threatened to spill anew from Zipporah's eyes. "The money is gone. My son must repay it with the labor of his hands."

"I can show him I care. That I am not blind to his hardship." She met his mother's swollen-eyed gaze. "Or yours."

Zipporah nodded. "My son…" a sob swallowed her response. "He traveled through the east gate, into the valley."

Blowing out a gale-wind breath, Adah leaned forward and kissed the grieving woman's veil. She recognized a familiar yet faint aroma of dust and ash. "*Toda raba*, my friend."

"Take our mule." The offer was uttered like a final plea. Zipporah struggled to rise. "He has been fed."

But not your son? Adah remembered the indentations under Othniel's ribs. She rallied compassion for Zipporah, but every muscle tensed. Othniel's parents had sold him like a slave. Could she forgive them? Could she forgive herself for standing around and watching his undoing? *God give me wisdom. How do I make this right?* Her stomach soured. What if she couldn't?

Micaiah marched to Adah's side. "I will harness

the mule and go with you."

She cast a glance at his mother for approval.

"He may go. He was asleep when his brother left." Zipporah wiped the wetness from her face. "At least I can say I provided an escort if your father challenges my discretion."

Basket grabbed and two feet from the door, Adah said, "I will pray for you and your household. You have suffered more than most. Now pray Othniel is weary of foot and my mule is fleet of hoof."

17

Micaiah pressed the basket against Adah's back as she guided the mule eastward, out of the city, through the valley, and in the direction of Hebron. Zipporah did not reveal Othniel's final destination, or if he would complete his journey in one day or many. Adah prayed he would stop in the border city before leaving the land promised to their forefathers.

She clenched the reins and did not flinch at the slight burn beneath her bandaged hand. How could Othniel's father agree to years of servitude for his son? If Othniel had shared his plight, she would have petitioned the rulers for a lighter tax burden. Why did men have to be so proud?

"Look for any lone travelers," she said to Micaiah. *Lord, help me find my friend.*

While the mule clopped onward, she willed Othniel to appear. He had to be found. She scanned the people on the road, searching for the confident, easy gait she had grown accustomed to having at her side.

Micaiah tapped her shoulder. "We should rest the animal." He pointed toward an oak tree off in the distance.

The shade beckoned, but a delay was her enemy. Although, if the mule pulled up lame they would never catch Othniel.

"Let's go a little farther before we rest." She prodded the mule onward and surveyed the road ahead.

Tugging on her garment, Micaiah said, "But the shade is here."

Her muscles wound tight like yarn on a spindle. *He's young and weary.* She blew out a breath. "Hold on and we'll trot over."

As they drew closer to the oak's drape of limbs and the shadowed ground beneath, a form camouflaged by the sprawling roots came into view.

"It's my brother." Micaiah wiggled like an unearthed worm. "Hurry!"

She kicked the mule and dipped under a low-lying branch, all the while her heart sped faster and faster. Could it be? Spying the form, her spirit soared. She knew that slumped head with its dark, unruly curls. If only she was lying beside him, feeling the tickle of his breath and the brush of his body.

Dismounting in an instant, she grabbed the basket from Micaiah and left him sitting high on top of the mule.

"Othniel." His name caught in her breaths. She knelt beside his bared calves, her knees skidding on the packed soil. "Wake up."

His eyes fluttered open.

She patted the side of his face. The bliss of finding her friend waned when she observed the haggard circles camped under his eyes. "You are weak. I have worked you too hard."

"You, no." He sat forward as if called to attention. "Telem, maybe." He tucked a wayward ringlet under her head covering.

Even though his touch was but a wisp of a caress, it awakened all of her senses.

"I would say I am dreaming, but I remember

scouting this tree for a short nap." His eyes held that hint of tease that she loved. "What are you doing so far from the city? You should not be here." He glanced about as if soldiers lay in wait.

"Of course I should." How could he think of her safety when he was the one sent from his home? She unfolded the cloth surrounding the bread. "I promised you something to eat. You rushed off without even saying farewell." She swallowed hard and tried to hide the hurt cinching her throat. Shaking her head, she said, "Now I am traipsing the desert to be true to my word."

He beheld her as if he truly thought she was a vision. "I know you too well." He stroked the weave of her basket, but the palm of his hand caressed her knee. "You would not be satisfied with my leaving."

Handing him a piece of bread, she said, "Then come back to me. I will do more. I should have done more. My father can persuade Rephaiah to lower your taxes."

"My father will not accept food from Shallum's table, nor a plea for leniency." He bit off a piece of bread. "What would happen the next time the taxes were due? Is my family to receive pity from another ruler?"

Micaiah approached slowly, as though he expected a reprimand from his brother.

Othniel reached out and waved him forward. "I should gift you silver, my brother, for protecting Adah. Come out of the sun and eat with us."

"You are not angry?" Micaiah focused his attention on an uncovered sweet cake.

"Of course not." Othniel finished the last of his bread. "Now I can thank you for doing my chores. By next year, you will be as tall as me."

"No." Micaiah shook his head. His dusty cheeks curved into a grin. "By the next moon."

A bold laugh burst forth from Othniel's chest. If only she could join in, but the thought of his absence was like a stone wedged against her heart. Her friend rose and hugged his younger brother, sending the boy off to the mule to fetch the larger waterskin.

"When will you return?" Her words were but a wisp. She shifted her weight onto her hip. Comfort would not stop the panic seizing her lungs.

Hands on hips, Othniel watched his brother untie the skin. "Six years. Micaiah may be betrothed by the time I return."

Six! The tide behind her eyes threatened to come to shore and stay. She was glad he did not turn around to bear witness to her grief. Why couldn't Othniel's family have bartered for one or two years of servitude?

"Where will you serve?" Jerusalem was the only answer that would settle her stomach.

"I go to Hebron and in a few days, to Kadesh-Barnea."

"Say it isn't so." She sprang to her feet. "One more step and you will be in Egypt." How could his father even consider such an arrangement? "The people to the south do not serve our God."

Othniel's stare became as unyielding as baked clay. "I only pray to the One True God." Adah beheld Othniel and his faith radiated from his stare. "I will mumble my prayers in my heart if need be. My family's honor is at stake. We must hold onto the land that has been passed down through generations. I do not intend to abandon my God."

Where was God? Why did He abandon Othniel?

And why did God withhold the rain? Couldn't He see how His people suffered?

The clatter of wooden cups and the trudge of Micaiah's sandals interrupted her troubled thoughts. Kneeling to pour drinks, the boy eyed the basket of food.

"Have a raisin cake." Othniel offered his brother the largest treat. "I only need a half. My path is away from the city. You may have to fight our enemies."

Even under the shade of the grand oak, heat swept through Adah's being. "What can I do?"

With a slight shake of his head, Othniel licked his lips and sipped the water his brother had brought.

She shifted closer and stood by his side. Othniel was present for the moment, and she would bathe in this cool shade with him now. "Tell me. I will petition even Nehemiah. Surely the governor could lower the burden on your family."

"And what of all the others struggling under the weight of the king's taxes? Can all the hardship be removed? My brothers must provide for their wives and Micaiah is too young to send away. I must serve so our land is secure." He swallowed the last of his drink and brushed his fingertips over her sleeve. "It is too late. You must carry on and build the wall. Honor your father's name as I honor my father's wishes. Be that brave and courageous woman who saved my vineyard."

His caress of her chin was but a brush of a breeze, but it thundered to her toes. Grasping his hand, she held it between them as if they were bound together. What would she do without Othniel's encouragement? Her chest pulled tighter than the leather atop a drum. "But you will be back." Her throat ached with every word spoken. "You cannot stay in a foreign land with foreign women."

"Tomorrow is not for certain, but I will always remember traipsing through the countryside with you." He lifted her necklace and fingered the beads. "You are my shining chrysolite gem, and I am your sandalwood."

"Don't say such a thing. You mean more to me than a thousand gems." She squeezed his clasped hand. "God will protect you, and you shall return to Jerusalem. To me."

"My future is not my own, I—"

"Are there more raisin cakes?" Micaiah asked, his eyes wide with anticipation.

She shook her head and gave a quivering smile. "I have some in Jerusalem."

Othniel slipped away and wrapped an arm around his brother's shoulder. "Take care of Adah and get her home safely." He scrubbed a hand over the boy's head wrap.

Adah turned away from the young boy's frantic embrace of his brother. Biting her tongue, she tried to keep the threads of her composure tightly knotted.

On the road, a caravan approached. The camels trudged in the direction Othniel headed. Her friend would travel safer with families around.

She picked up the cloth with the uneaten bread inside. Oh how she wished she could place a feast in his basket. Instead, she removed a pouch of cinnamon from her belt and added it. Not only would it flavor his bread, but just maybe it would remind him of her.

"You must take this food." She concentrated on her friend's need for nourishment and not on Micaiah's ruddy face. Her hands shook as she fumbled the flap of

Othniel's satchel. "I made this for you."

Looking up as he helped her place the bread in his leather pack, their gazes met and lingered. How could she have been so short of sight? All the time they had spent together crossing streams and groves in search of new blooms and new scents, her greatest find was standing right in front of her.

"You are my fragrant flower," he whispered.

"I will wait for you." Her reasoning rushed forth in a desperate plea. "I will talk with my father..."

He pressed a finger to her lips. "And your father will not allow it. Not with all the uncertainty. What can I offer a ruler's daughter?"

"Everything." A tear branded her cheek. "We must believe God will act."

"You must believe. Finish the wall, so one day if I return I can tell anyone who will listen how we stacked those stones." With a quick glance toward the caravan, he kissed her forehead. "*Shalom.*"

Before she could reply, he sprinted southward, joining the procession of wagons, animals, and travelers.

Adah gripped her empty basket and squeezed her eyes shut, branding the caress of his lips into her memory. Never once did Othniel turn around. And never once did she try and stop him.

18

Shouts of masons and the thud of hammers greeted Adah as she neared Jerusalem. No relief crept into her soul at seeing the growth of the wall and the frame of the gates. Her posture grew rigid every time she thought of Othniel running to join strangers on his journey to serve a foreign master. Why build Jerusalem and make her a fortress, only to sell her people to slave in the lands of their enemies? She had kept Nehemiah's secret about the assembly, but today she would not stay silent about the injustice around her.

"Forgive me, Lord," she prayed. "For I passed by Beulah's grief as if it were a bother. Now the same suffering has come upon my heart, and I cannot ignore the pain. Embolden me to speak for the downtrodden."

After entering the city, she dismounted and withdrew her sword from the saddle bag before sending Micaiah on his way with the mule. If Othniel's father would not accept choice meats from the daughter of Shallum, perhaps he would accept fodder for the mount she had ridden. She would send a supply of hay for the mule later and wrap some raisin cakes for Micaiah.

Marching toward the council chambers, she passed the temple, and dodged a few stragglers returning from afternoon prayer. An overhang held up by four thin columns cast shade on the steps to the meeting place. A mosaic of indigo and amber tiles outlined the main entrance. As she reached for the door, it flung open. Nehemiah nearly trampled her. She jumped backward as the governor and Ezra halted. The aroma of sage and myrtle incense wafted from the room the priest and Nehemiah had just left.

"Daughter of Shallum." Nehemiah's eyes widened at her presence. "You are not working on the wall today?"

"Governor. Teacher." She bowed and nodded toward Ezra. "If you will hear me, I have a case to plead." Wiping her hands together, she willed the worn strip of bandage to soak up her sweat.

"May it never be said that I did not listen to one who gave me comfort in a time of grief." The governor turned to Ezra. "I do not want to keep you from your duties."

"By all means, allow the woman to speak. She still carries that sword." Ezra encouraged her with a thin-lipped grin.

She clasped her hands to keep them from shaking and cleared her throat. Oh how she prayed the governor would be as willing to hear her rebuke as he had been to receive her comfort. "You once told me you followed God's leading and petitioned the king to leave the palace and rebuild the wall where your fathers lie buried."

"I did." Nehemiah's gruff response nearly turned her feet to stone.

"Aren't we building a wall to protect our city and our people? Yet these rocks cannot protect us against famine. These boulders cannot stop our sons and daughters from being sent away to serve in pagan households. Families who cannot pay their taxes are forfeiting their children for a few coins." Her attention fell to Ezra. "Doesn't our law forbid this slavery?"

The priest arched his back. Had she insulted his knowledge?

"Who has sanctioned the servitude of our people? Certainly, not I." He cast a glance at the governor. "I have been diligent in upholding God's commands."

Adah tensed. She did not intend to insult Ezra, but she knew of what she spoke. She looked to Nehemiah, confident in their friendship.

Nehemiah gazed out over the sun-drenched steps. "I have not been here long. But my desire is to fill these streets, not empty them." He crossed his arms and tapped a rhythm with his fingers. "Let us ask the rulers about such a matter. They are the ones that settle the debts of our people."

Shuffling sandals caught her attention. If she had been a bird, she would have flown high into the sky, for at that moment, her father, followed by Rephaiah and his hateful son Gershom, sauntered toward the governor. They hiked the steps and stopped, closing off any way of escape. Ezra widened their intimate circle.

Caught in a vice between powerful men, she stiffened. *Be brave and courageous.*

"Shallum. Rephaiah." The governor's call upon the rulers held no hint of pleasantries. "Is hardship causing our people to stray from the Law? Have we not tended to the poor? Your daughter has brought a serious charge against the officials of this city."

Her father's face wrinkled. He glared at her with a fierceness she had only seen when the doctors testified her mother would never regain her sight. "Daughter, what is this gossip? What falsehoods have the laborers been spreading?"

The condemnation in her father's voice chilled her blood. When did she ever stand idle and whisper half-truths? "Father." She reminded him of their kinship. "Othniel is on his way to Kadesh-Barnea so his family can pay taxes on their fields. He is bound for six years to an idol worshipper."

"How can this be?" Ezra said, stroking his beard and perusing the officials. "Was this suffering brought before an elder or a priest?"

Gershom laughed like a braying donkey while his father remained stiff and still. "She is lovesick." Gershom swished his hand as if a sudden swarm of gnats attacked his position. "Her man leaves her and she petitions us to bring him back. Dismiss her accusation. Work is not a hardship for a boy. Why are we to blame if his family did not manage their obligations?"

Flames licked every nerve in Adah's body. "Where is your compassion for those who labor on cursed soil? Can a landowner summon the rain? You jingle coins in your pouches earned from their sweat while people go hungry and mourn for sacrificed children."

"Sacrificed?" Rephaiah gripped the drape of his cloak. "Do not compare our ways with those of godless heathens."

"We may not throw babies into the fire to please foreign gods, but we are selling our sons and daughters into servitude so a few can prosper. Can we all not bear the tax burden on this city and share food from our tables?" Her throat stung from the force of her truth-filled words.

"Shallum, silence your daughter," Rephaiah

shouted. He nearly knocked his own turban from his head. "I have heard enough of these lies. Am I unjust in my duties?"

Her father gripped her arm with an unknown ferocity. Beads of perspiration shone on his face. "This is not the place for insults. Leave us."

She ripped free from her father's grasp and beheld Nehemiah. He stood in the shade of the overhang as grand and tall as the columns. "Governor, please. Today I saw a God-fearing man leave this city. How many more will follow with a drought cursing our lands?"

"You have been deceived. There is no crime in working to pay a tax." Her father tugged her closer to the steps and away from the meeting room door. "I have confidence Rephaiah considered this matter and reached a fair understanding with the landowners."

Like he faithfully handled the news of Nehemiah's arrival? She knew a message had come regarding the governor's plans, but Rephaiah had hidden the information from her father. Firsthand she had seen how his son mocked the landowner's pleas for assistance. Their deceptions would not reign victorious this day.

She resisted the pull of her father and locked her gaze on Nehemiah. "People are living in poverty. They're unable to feed their children. I know this to be true." Rounding on her father, she said, "What about our own neighbor, Beulah? Have you not seen the tears she spills over her daughter's absence."

Her father scowled, beholding her as if she were demon-possessed and frothing at the mouth.

"Our own neighbor grieves a daughter sent away so her unborn baby can be fed." She gaped at her father's indifference. "Tell me you are not blind to Beulah's misery."

Whap. Pain ricocheted across her cheek. Shocked, she cupped her jaw and swallowed blood-tainted spit. She bore this insult with a furious humility, for who knew what abuse awaited Othniel or Beulah's daughter.

Her father shook, his garment trembling from the collar to its hem. "We are well aware of the hardship this drought has caused. It is not your place to question our rule."

Someone must. For all the ones who can't speak. She let her hand fall to her side. *God, where are You?*

"Woe to you, woman, for suggesting you know better than a man." Rephaiah stomped his foot and clapped a hand on her father's shoulder. "It is about time you disciplined such a reckless girl."

With a throbbing face, she turned toward Nehemiah and Ezra, and nodded, showing her respect. "I have spoken the truth about our people's struggles. I'm sorry I wasn't emboldened sooner. God has entrusted you with the oversight of our people." She eyed her father. "You men, do as you see fit. May God grant you wisdom. *Shalom.*"

She navigated the steps with her head held high and a hand on her sword. A few people waiting nearby muttered as she passed. Ramming through the streets like a bull on a charge, she arrived at her family's designated station along the wall. Pine-scented pitch burned her nostrils.

Telem pounded a stone with vigor. "Where are all my workers? The brothers must keep one eye on the wilderness. Some sentry you are. A legion could have swept in against us."

Humiliated by her father, and with an ache in her jaw, she glowered at the mason. For the first time in their short acquaintance, he actually shut his mouth and returned his attention to shifting rock.

19

She didn't know how long she stood in place watching Telem toil against the weight of a boulder. She did not care to move. An anchor may as well have chained her to this spot.

Where should she go after such a humiliating encounter with her father? A confrontation witnessed by the governor of Judah. Should she go out to search for Jehu and relieve him as a guard? Should she stay and help her mason? Part of her wanted to run to her storeroom and mix perfumes, leaving this project of Nehemiah's to the men. She could easily lift a jug of oil or chop henna blossoms. Fitting rock and securing cornerstones were foreign skills. But she had answered the governor's call before the priests and her neighbors, and ultimately before God. Tongues would gossip about her absence after the commotion on the steps. Several people had not only seen but also heard her father's slap.

Generations would know that Shallum and his daughters built this section of the wall. Did she and Judith not seek out Telem? Did they not labor where they could? They would finish this task they had begun, even if neighbors watched and whispered, their glances betraying their distaste of women working alongside men of no relation.

Adah lifted her face toward the afternoon sun and sighed. So much had changed in the previous hours.

With Othniel. With her father. Within her. She did not want to share these emotions of betrayal, embarrassment, and love, but she owed her mason an explanation as to where his workers had gone, so she put her feelings in an imaginary jar and capped it with poplar wood.

When her breathing calmed, she spoke. "My father is meeting with the governor. And Othniel." She swallowed hard to keep her emotions from warbling her words. "He will not be returning to help us." Biting the fleshy inside of her cheek, she battled the tingle of tears demanding to reappear.

Telem crouched and inspected the wall for gaps. "I gathered as much."

She shook her head. "What do you mean?" Othniel had only left this morning.

"The boy's father came by while you were guarding the rubble. They argued."

"You listened?"

"I heard." Telem stood. "I am all over this area." He indicated his tools scattered about.

Frustration pulsed through her temples. "You could have warned me."

"It was not my place."

"He worked with you!"

"And he worked for you." Telem studied her with a gaze so dark and deep she could have jumped in and disappeared. "You are not a fool, Adah. He worked for more than a debt."

"I believe I was a fool. For I never thought he would be taken away." Pressure pounded behind her eyes. "Not in the way he was. Sent to serve in a foreign land." She picked up a stick to stir the pitch pot. "Selling our people is against the Law."

"I know the Law. And when I departed from it, I suffered." He shuffled closer. "When I lived in the cave, I didn't have to see people in need. Now, it seems, there is need all around us."

She halted her stirring stick and leaned upon it. "My conscience is clear. I told the governor and all the rulers about Othniel…and of another sold for taxes and food."

"That is the meeting your father attends?" Telem burst forth in a laugh and sent a raven soaring from a scraggly tree. "The faster you receive Jehu's cloak and blend in with the rocks, the better." He stilled her stirring. "Remember, God sees everything. He sees our sins, but he also sees our offerings." Pulling the stick from her clutch, he said, "The One True God knows our hearts, and you have a good heart, daughter of Shallum. Now go relieve Jehu and keep us safe."

"*Toda raba.* Your praise is like a balm on my wounds." She glanced around to see if her sister neared. "What about Judith?"

"She took your mother to wash, and I believe they will return with a meal." Telem's lips pressed together as if he withheld a smile. "Do not worry. I will take care of her."

"And you will take care of the food she brings." Adah would not have believed Telem had a carefree demeanor unless she had witnessed it with her own eyes. Was returning to Jerusalem healing his old wounds? She had all night to ponder such things. If only Othniel was around to hear her thoughts.

"Off with you." Telem's voice awakened her from her daydream. He stalked toward the water jar. "Find Jehu and relieve him from his post. I need another man to labor."

If only it were the last time she heard that sentiment. "As you wish."

She turned toward the length of the wall that ran south and bordered the Valley Gate. She knew the length by memory after one night of walking back and forth from her father's section to the priests' section. But somehow this night felt different, as if she was a lone tower of bricks and her scaffolding had been removed before the work was finished. Keeping Jerusalem safe meant something to her, as it did to Nehemiah and Othniel. Although, one of them would not be here to rejoice when the work was complete. Her conscience ached with that knowledge.

As the setting sun left a haze of simmering scarlet flames, it revealed the silhouette of low lying segments of the wall that lagged in repair behind other areas of the city. She found Jehu leaning against a tower of bricks that Telem had mortared. His cloak lay folded near his post.

Jehu shaded his eyes. "You are early. I can still see your face."

"Not for long, and Telem needs you more than he does me."

"I am not so sure about that." He handed her his cloak. "I do not envy you. The priests squabble like hens. Hanun has been shouting all afternoon. May they take a rest and allow you some peace."

They cannot give me peace. She held up his garment. "*Shalom.* I will tie my veil around my ears."

Jehu nodded and trudged off to seek Telem.

"Stars, come swiftly," she prayed.

She found a small gap in the wall and peered at the outskirts of the city. A light breeze cooled her swathed body. Palms and tamarisk trees rebuffed the wind, their fronds and branches barely moving.

"Are you happy, God?" She breathed in the scent of fire pit smoke. Usually the aroma of burning oak and acacia ash soothed her soul, but this night, she stood restless. "This is what You wanted. A renewed fortress. A fortified city. A new Jerusalem."

When the rocks at her side made impressions in her arm, she shifted. Star-lit shadows blanketed the brush. Thankfully, the moon held court over the city, easing the strain on her eyes. A faint odor of clove oil reminded her of her healing palm, but mostly the aroma reminded her of Othniel's caress. *Take care of him, Lord.*

A sentry further down sauntered toward the Valley Gate.

She waited and glanced toward his spot a time or three.

Stepping outside her post, she shuffled over uneven dirt and up an embankment to glimpse the length of the southern wall. Where had the sentry gone? Priests labored on the frame of the gate. She even heard a song of praise to God.

Farther south, on a path to the Dung Gate, donkeys labored to pull two wagons. Tarps covered the wagon beds and tented over the load. Were these wagons dumping dung at the far gate? Or were they delayed merchants rounding the city for an eastern gate?

A torch held by a companion of the lead driver served as a bright beacon to the wagon in the rear. Was this a family and the torchbearer a wife? Wrapped like a Bedouin in a dust storm, the wife of the front merchant hunched forward and pulled back the hood of her cloak.

And spit. Was that a beard shadowing her face?

A chill cascaded down Adah's back. That wife was no woman. Adah would know, for she was not a man.

20

Adah darted toward the south gates, careful not to twist her ankle on the rocks, mortar pebbles, and sticks strewn around the outside of the wall. Her breaths came in gasps and pants. Her throat burned. She leapt over the low lying mortared stones. Hanun's kin met her entry with wide-eyed disbelief, dumbstruck that a woman halted their labors.

No one challenged her intrusion. No blades were drawn. Had her people so soon forgotten the armies who had challenged Nehemiah? Perhaps it was her oversized cloak and her unruly, half-covered hair giving these men of Judah a start.

"Soldiers are heading toward the Dung Gate. Hiding in wagons." Her chest heaved as she blurted her warning. "We must sound the shofar and alert our people."

A broad-shouldered laborer assessed her chipped toenails and windblown ringlets. "You're a woman." He waved her off. "We have guards posted. Why do our brothers not come with this news?"

Her heart flogged her chest and sent a loud boom echoing from one ear to the other. "I am disguised to fool our enemies." She tugged on the hood of her cloak. "Would you let them do the same to us? I saw a man swathed in veils pretending to be a wife. Do not let these false women be your undoing." Gesturing wildly toward the Dung Gate, she said, "Soldiers are hiding in those wagons. *Bevakasha.* Listen. Follow me.

It is only a short run. I know, for my father oversees this part of the city." She scanned the group of men, meeting every laborer's stare. "I will not stay silent about danger to my city."

"We've all heard rumors of attacks." The broad leader assessed his fellow workers. "We will take heed. "He pointed to the laborers closest to the wall. "Stay and defend this section." With a sigh, he turned toward the others and patted his blade. "The rest, come with me and the girl. If this is a trick of war, we will meet the enemy."

Thank you, Lord.

She warned everyone laboring in her path as she dodged around campfires and maneuvered past axes and mallets strewn on the ground. "Be brave and courageous," she called out to the small band of fighting men who believed her story and followed after her. "God will act."

Will you act this time God? Confuse our enemy? Halt their evil?

When she reached the southern entrance to her city, only a few men labored on the wall abutting the Dung Gate. The stench of animal waste hung in the air. Less than half a dozen priests stood watch. Why weren't more men securing this entry? Jerusalem had no wooden doors to keep out the wicked.

"Warn these workers," she huffed to her muscled neighbor. "We must sound a horn."

His strides slowed. "If you're certain."

"I am." She bent at the waist to control her breathing. "I most definitely am."

Rising and arching her back, she spied Delaiah, a priest, on the other side of the small clearing inside the Dung Gate. He drank from a tall water jar. A ram's horn hung from his shoulder.

She sprinted across the wide entryway, her throat burning, her lips parched. Catching sight of the donkeys lumbering closer to the gate, she petitioned God to intervene. *Do not forsake us, Lord.* Yellow-orange torch flames from the first wagon taunted her prayers.

"Delaiah, sound the shofar," she rasped, coming upon the imbibing priest.

The temple official sputtered and spilled water on his tasseled robe. His contempt bore down on her. "What is the meaning of this interruption?" He gripped the horn at his hip as though she were a thief and the trumpet was cast of pure gold and in need of protection.

"Those wagons are full of soldiers." She lowered her voice to keep the enemy ignorant.

Fixing his gaze on the wagon master and his shrouded wife, Delaiah scowled. "Nothing is out of the ordinary. You would have me cause an uproar and distress our governor over a few late travelers?"

"Yes!" She balled her hands into fists and beat the air like a drum. The lead wagon was breaching the gate.

He backed away from her shrill affirmation and flailing hands. "You are the daughter of Shallum." He jabbed a finger at her nose. "The governor has called a meeting because of your false accusations."

She didn't care if this holy man held her in disregard. At this moment, her home and her people were in danger. She would act the mad woman to save the City of David from destruction. Lunging, she gripped the shofar and drew it toward her face.

Before she could place her lips on the mouthpiece, Delaiah clawed after his precious horn, scratching her chin. He grasped her perfumer's necklace and twisted. His fist crushed her throat.

Her eyes bulged. Gagging, she jerked away. Sandalwood and chrysolite beads sailed into the darkness.

Hands still on the horn, she yanked it closer to her lips. One gust of breath was all she needed to alert her people.

Delaiah stepped forward. His strap went slack. The horn struck her teeth. Hands on her shoulders, he shoved her to the ground with the force of an enraged bull. As she attempted to rise, wooden orbs from her necklace embedded in her palm.

Sneering, the priest *tsked* a reprimand. "Your father will hear of this lack of respect." He shifted the shofar behind his body and kicked at her sandals.

Her father's rebuke was the least of her worries. If she did not warn the people, someone could die. "Sound the trumpet," she screamed. She would not allow the second wagon to enter her city.

Shaking his head, Delaiah continued drinking.

Righting herself, she spied grass growing from the base of the waist-high watering jars. She bent and picked the longest blade of grass visible in the dim light. Othniel had serenaded her with long leaves before. Placing the blade lengthwise between her thumbs, she pressed her knuckles together, cupped her hands, and blew. A squeaking rumble erupted into the night. She blew over and over so the ghastly whine centered all attention on the crazed woman with the whistle.

"Draw your swords." She unsheathed her weapon and pointed the tip at the wagon driver. Her lips still hummed with the vibrations of her reed. "Our enemies are upon us. Wield a sword for the Lord!"

Flying into the air, the tarp released armed warriors into the courtyard. Rolling off the cart, foreigners engaged in battle with the closest Hebrew.

Delaiah sounded the shofar.

At last! Praise the Lord! The second wagon remained on the road outside the city.

Shouts. Cries. Clanging. War overpowered the routine clinks of the masons at work. Dust clouded the air. Jittery donkeys attempted a retreat away from the fight.

Adah needed to retreat as well, away from a bloodthirsty enemy.

A foreigner broke free from the chaos and charged her direction. His blade was curved and ready to kill.

Adah raised her sword. Hands trembling, the weapon wavered. How could she pierce her enemy's studded-leather breastplate? Delaiah drew a jagged-edged knife. Its sharpness may have slit a goat's throat for temple offerings, but their foe's weapon went unmatched.

If you won't act, God, then I will. She shoved the waist-high drinking jar. Water flooded the sun-dried soil. Shining chrysolite gems bobbed in the small river. Her assailant stomped one sandaled foot and then a second and slipped and crashed into a thin layer of mud.

"Retreat," she shouted at the ruthless man. Her heartbeat boomed with the command. "Don't make me kill you."

A broad-shouldered builder appeared sword at the ready. "I don't mind." He impaled their enemy with a two-handed thrust of his blade. Blood splattered and wet the ground.

Cupping her mouth, Adah heaved. Her throat burned. Her tongue tasted like sour raisins.

Crack! The spooked donkeys wedged their wagon lengthwise across the frame of the gate, narrowing the path of escape for the spies. Grunting subsided. Enemy soldiers retreated and scaled the cart, rushing to freedom. Their cowardly forms faded into the shadows of the wilderness.

"Check the wall," her surly priest commanded to the nearest laborers. "Protect any openings." If only he had used this voice earlier for a warning.

Men from the city advanced into the clearing from nearby streets. Nehemiah rode toward her atop one of the king's horses.

With her fellow Judahites, she ran along the inside of the wall, dodging bodies of fallen fighters face down in the dirt. Any testimony required of her would have to wait. She had to get back to her post and see about her sister, Telem, and the brothers.

As she neared the tower of stones where she had kept watch, a woman's frantic shrieks stood out from the male voices awakening the night. Judith? Adah's cheeks flamed. Was her sister injured? She shot through the opening in the wall.

A short distance away, she saw him, by the pitch pot, face up on the ground. It was Telem. Fresh blood seeped into the woven threads of his tunic. Her twin sister clawed at her long dark hair and hovered over their fallen mason.

"No," Adah wailed. It can't be. It just can't be. She stumbled and dropped to her knees by Telem's side.

"Where were you?" Judith's blade quaked in her hands. "The enemy came right through the wall."

21

Adah cupped Telem's face in her hands. She was a fool to leave her friends. Not only did the enemy soldiers breech the Dung Gate, they also sneaked undetected into the city from the second wagon and laid siege to the low-lying areas of the wall. *Lord, why was I the one who had to spy their deception?*

"Forgive me," she said to her mason. Now was not the time to explain the reason she abandoned her post. Telem's wound needed to be closed. She swallowed the spit pooling in her mouth and willed her stomach not to empty. In the intimate space, it smelled like a calf had been butchered. "Did the blade go all the way through?"

"Can't look." Telem grimaced. He held Judith's head covering over the puncture. "I am dizzy when I lift my head."

"No. No it didn't." Judith's eyes were as big as walnuts. "I did not see the tip, and I was at his back. Jehuliel had called for me to return."

"Praise God he did." She motioned to the brothers who stood slack-jawed near the fire. "Grab a mat or a blanket. We must get him to our home. Hurry!"

Adah sprang to her feet and untied her sword. "Take this," she said to a laborer perched on the wall. "Keep watch. If so much as a mouse scurries over the wall, slay it."

The man regarded her as if she was possessed, but

he accepted the weapon with a gleam in his eye.

Judith's head and shoulders swayed to an imaginary song. Adah hurried to her sister's side and patted her cheeks. "Run home and find me a needle and thread. Have a servant warm some water. Do you hear?"

Judith nodded, tears staining her cheeks. She stumbled toward their dwelling.

Jehu and Jehuliel maneuvered a blanket under her mason.

"We will need a jug of wine too," Adah called after her sister.

"Are you celebrating?" Telem rasped.

"Later. When you can join us." Adah's smile trembled. She placed pressure on the soaked veil. "Piercing your skin will be painful."

"I don't think it can get any worse." He trembled as the brothers shifted his torso.

"Think again. The best seamstress in our household is my blind mother."

Telem groaned.

Adah jogged to keep up with the brothers as they carried Telem through the streets. "Move aside," she shouted to anyone in their path. Her hand stayed flat upon Telem's chest, forcing his lifeblood to stay inside his body.

Guilt clung to her like a wet garment. "I'm so sorry, Telem. I should never have left my post and gone to the gate."

"If you had stayed. You would be dead." His head rolled to the side. "How," he released a few short breaths, "could I tell your mother I allowed it?"

"My mother knows how persuasive I can be. If sighted, she would have joined me in guarding the

city. This is our home." Now was not the time to argue her reason for standing sentry.

As they approached her home, the door whipped open. Judith stood just beyond the threshold.

"We have cleared an area in the front room." Her twin sister held up threaded metal. "I have mother's embroidery needle."

"It's bent like a hook," Adah said while the brothers gently lowered Telem to the floor.

Her mother, hand to the wall, shuffled closer. "You will never close the skin with a straight one. Flesh is too thick."

The ground beneath Adah's feet began to roll like the sea. Blood stained her fingers, hands, and arms. Blood. Everywhere. Blood. "God of Jacob give me strength and skill," she muttered.

Adah sat next to Telem on the floor. She clenched her teeth and blinked like she was caught in a dust storm. *Lord, get me through this.* Judith handed her the threaded needle.

Lifting the soiled rag from Telem's wound, she beheld the sword's damage, and swiftly pinched the skin together. Sweat dampened her forehead. "I was never the best at sewing."

"Unfortunately, it was a skill I possessed." Her mother braced herself against the wall, her face drawn as if she could see the injury. "You will do fine. It's a simple pattern."

Judith pressed a cup to Telem's lips. "Drink. You've braved enough pain."

"Begin then." Telem clenched his teeth. "Before I become accustomed to it." His head fell backward and he faced the ceiling.

Adah pierced Telem's skin with a quick thrust. His

flesh was solid. A bubble of blood oozed from her puncture. Her body chilled. *Be strong.* She looped the thread and pulled it tight, but not too tight to overlap the skin. She tied it. Knotted it. One stitch was finished. A drop of water snaked down the side of her face.

When she jabbed Telem again, his back arched slightly. Judith offered more wine. The scent of salted meat set Adah's throat ablaze. She swallowed fast and hard. Thankfully, she hadn't eaten much since the bread and cake she shared with Othniel. *Be courageous.* She continued, stitch after stitch, closing Telem's wound until it no longer gave up fresh blood.

Judith faced Adah, lips moving, but with no prayers spoken out loud.

Adah splayed her bloodstained fingers. "Sister, I need you to go to my workshop. Bring me turmeric. Mother will have honey." She could not allow redness and swelling to set into Telem's flesh.

Her sister nodded and hurried toward the door.

"First row on the shelf. Fourth jar," Adah said.

"Am I a delicacy?" Telem's booming voice was but a vapor.

She should tease him and say no, but his suffering was the result of helping her fulfill a vow. With tears threatening to spill, she said, "Yes. I don't know where I would be if you had stayed in your cave."

"It seems God has blessed us both." He swallowed. "And Adah," he continued.

Leaning in close to hear her mason's words, she placed her unclean hand on a soiled rag.

"Have your sister care for me while I recover." Telem closed his eyes. A hint of a grin lingered on his rugged face.

Adah sat back and stared.

If she hadn't fought the enemy with her own sword, Adah would have believed Telem had planned his own injury so he could receive Judith's attention. She dabbed his skin with a clean cloth. Would her sister consider Telem suitable for a husband?

"Daughter, you must wash." Her mother received a folded tunic and veil from a servant. We will burn your garments and forget this night. I can help your sister tend to Telem's skin."

"Yes, let us forget this day." She thought of Othniel. She didn't even know where he laid his head this night. Would his presence at their station have kept Telem from being wounded? Or would he have been struck down defending the city? Her cheeks grew hot. Pressure tingled behind her eyes. It was no use crying. She had spoken her peace about the injustice to the governor, the rulers, and her father. What was done could not be undone.

She went outside into the cooking courtyard to wash off Telem's blood. Her mother's servant followed carrying unstained clothing. Thankfully, a sheet hung in the back corner to dry. She could change unnoticed.

Other servants had filled jars with water for cleansing—water that would need to be dumped outside the city once it had turned the color of a tuberose.

When her skin was clean and her dress did not reek of death, she hurried out from behind the sheet to check on Telem and Judith. This cursed day could not end soon enough.

"There she is," a man's voice called.

Her father and that fool of a priest Delaiah strode down the street in her direction.

She left the courtyard and greeted them.

Delaiah pointed a finger at her face. His other hand rested on the ram's horn slung from his shoulder. "This is the wild woman who attacked me."

22

Adah gaped at the priest. How could he insult her in front of her father?

The men blocked her return to her home. They stood with wide stances, their hands on their hips, forming a fortress with their bodies. Her civility hung by one thin fiber after the bloodshed this night. How could Delaiah call her lawless after she'd had to force him to protect his own city? How many more of her people would have died if she did not blow on a reed and scream a warning?

Lord, give me strength. I need to get back to Telem and back to the wall.

"Father," she said, straightening her posture as if giving a defense before a judge. "I believe my actions were misunderstood. I did not strike my elder or touch his skin." She met the priest's stare and withheld the urge to grab his adorned robe and shake the truth from his lips. "I pleaded with him to sound his trumpet and warn our men that the enemy was near."

"You kept me from doing my duty." Her accuser leaned forward and spoiled the night air with his fermented wheat breath. "Shallum, your daughter ran past the gate in a man's robe and confused my guards with her shrieks."

"Your guards? There weren't enough men at the gate to water mules." She took a step toward her father to explain her actions. "I saw wagons entering our city and wondered why merchants would travel at such a late hour. Then I saw a man in disguise and knew this was a trick of our enemies."

Her father's brow furrowed as he thumbed his beard "Weren't you with Telem?" His question held a hint of surprise.

She ignored Delaiah's pious smirk. Hadn't her father praised the rise of their section of the wall? Surely he knew she and Judith weren't lifting rocks at heights far above their heads? She would not hide the truth. "I was standing sentry at a low section of the wall so Telem could work."

"Hah!"

The priest's self-righteous snort curled her hands into fists. "Isn't that what Nehemiah ordered?" She beheld her father and willed his understanding, for he stood as unmoving as a baked clay vessel. "I had a sharp sword to defend myself and this city."

"A city which you stepped out of in the dark of night and fled to the priests at the gate accompanied by men who were of no relation." Her father stated the charge like he had heard it thrice before.

What male relation should she have called? She had no brothers or cousins or uncles. Should she have ignored what she saw? Waited on God to foil the attempt? What if God had abandoned Jerusalem once and for all? Nehemiah didn't believe that and neither did she. God protected the city because a woman dressed in a man's robe witnessed a man dressed as a woman acting unladylike.

This time it was her turn to thrust her shoulders back, puff out her chest and dig her fists into her hips. "I sounded a warning to save our people."

"I could have sounded the shofar if you didn't

distract me." Delaiah jabbed his finger close to her eye.

"But you wouldn't." Her charge rattled the rooftops.

Her father stepped between her and the overbearing temple servant. "No one was killed in the raid. We have a few wounded fighters. One being my own mason."

Was that all her father had to say about her heroics? Did he believe the shaded truth of this man over his own daughter? She stepped back and rubbed her arms, trying to warm her skin from the cold shroud that suddenly draped over her. No matter how hard she tried to impress her father, she would never bring him as much honor as a son.

"You must do something about her, Shallum. If she is not put in her place, all women will think they can act like a man. That girl confronted her elders and the governor as if she had authority. She spoke out of turn in public. Ran through the streets with a sword. This shamefulness must stop."

Adah praised God that her father was a wall between the priest and herself, for if no person stood between them, she would have been tempted to speak her mind.

She placed a hand upon her father's shoulder and swallowed the rage that caused her body to tremble. She clenched her jaw as the priest came back into view.

"I am sorry you did not feel my actions were helpful to you or to this city, but I took a vow to help restore Jerusalem's wall before my father, my governor, and my God. And unless my father forbids me from continuing with my labors, I will work alongside men who are not my relation. They are solely my people."

Delaiah flapped his arms. "Shallum—"

"You heard my daughter. As a man of the law, you know there is nothing I can do about her vow after all this time has passed. I did not disavow her at the assembly." Her father sounded almost as if he wished he had rejected her plans to restore the wall and have his name written in the record books. "I think it best we return to our duties and prepare for our meeting with the governor tomorrow."

The priest cast a squinty-eyed glare upon her. "We all know who is responsible for that insult."

Adah blew out a silent breath, thankful her father did not rebuke her labors at the wall or chastise her for Nehemiah's summons. She bowed to relieve the cramping in her stomach and hoped the show of respect would slow the slander of her name. "My mason is not well. I need to prepare herbs for a dressing."

With a nod, she hurried across the street to her storeroom. Once inside, she leaned against the door and basked in the aroma of familiar blossoms, tangy fruits, and earthy moss. Enough moonlight seeped through the window and she didn't bother to light a lamp. Every jar and bottle had its place, and she knew the precise location of each one.

The cupboard door hung open. In her rush for turmeric, Judith had probably left it ajar. Adah reached toward the top shelf for lavender oil and halted. There, gawking at her, with its tapered tail and embedded dirt eyes was the wooden lizard Othniel had rescued from the stream. Her eyes tingled with tears. He was gone. Had he only left hours ago when it seemed like many Sabbaths?

Don't cry.

"Protect my Othniel," she prayed. "I love him." Uttering those last words gave her weary limbs new life to perform her tasks. With Telem wounded, Jehu and Jehuliel would need her help all the more.

When her jars of healing oils were gathered and organized in a basket, a droplet of water snaked from her thigh to the side of her knee. She shivered as the wetness eased down her calf.

Moving backward for a better glow of moonlight, she lifted her hem and glanced at her ankle.

Blood. Oh no, not her flow.

"Why now, Lord? Haven't I done enough?" She faced the ceiling. "I am not a man, nor do I want to be, but this is the worst possible time to be a woman. An unclean woman." How could she help take care of Telem if she couldn't touch him, or anyone else without making them unclean and in need of isolation?

She reached for her necklace to count the beads and calm her spirit, but when her fingers stroked her neck, all she felt was bare skin.

23

A woman with her monthly flow was avoided and feared lest a tap of a finger or the brush of her garment caused someone to be unclean and ostracized for a day. Six more suns would have to set before Adah could leave the temporary isolation of her storeroom. Wiping the dust from her work table, she chased the shadows of another sinking sun with every sweep of her cloth. She didn't have time to sit idle. And by now, gossip would have flooded the city. Her altercation at the gate and her absence from the wall would make an intoxicating whisper. But better her seclusion than another scandal from touching someone and making them unclean for a night.

She sighed as she reclined on a stool and closed her eyes to pray. *Lord, give me relief from my distress. Be merciful to me and hear my prayer. Remember my father as he oversees the city. Heal Telem's wound that he may work again on Jerusalem's wall. Walk beside Othniel in a foreign land. I want to be brave and do your work, but all it has brought me is sorrow and scorn. Why do you not protect your people?*

She forgot to breathe and tightness consumed her chest.

"Adah?" Judith knocked on the threshold and entered carrying a basket. The aroma of warm bread wafted into the room.

"You are late." Adah rose. Her stomach stirred at

the welcome scent of food. How could she have snapped at her sister who brought her meal? She softened her demeanor and plucked a grape from its stem. "Has Telem been an injured bear?"

"Perhaps with the servants, but not with me." A plum-colored blush crossed her sister's cheeks. "He is thankful for my attention."

"There are no signs of festering? His skin is not red?"

"He complains I am seasoning a stew with all your oils." Judith placed Adah's meal on the table. "But otherwise he is kind and grateful. No cross words has he spoken. His skin looks no worse than before, save the stitching."

Adah scanned the basket for a small pouch "I am glad. Perhaps his angry words are only meant for me."

"Because you do not listen to him." Judith crossed her arms and leaned against the table.

"Well, we will have several days apart to practice our patience." Adah pressed her lips together, and frowned. "You did not find my beads at the gate?"

Judith shook her head. "Not a one. I even moved some of the watering jars."

"The chrysolite might tempt a thief, but who would want to steal small round bits of wood?" Adah broke off a piece of bread and sighed. "Mother gave me that necklace when I made my first fragrance."

"I am sorry I did not find a few beads, sister." Judith snapped her fingers. "I must be tired, for I forgot your drink." She hesitated in the threshold. "I am sorry, too, for blaming you for Telem's injuries. I did not know about the wagons until that priest accused you of helping the enemy."

"You were in shock after the attack." Adah

slumped against the corner of her work table. "And to think you had to hear that priest's lies."

"How could I not? He shrieked like a newborn." Judith rubbed her eyes with her fists and wailed like a babe.

"I would embrace you if the law allowed." Adah grinned at her elder sister. Judith may have entered the world only a few minutes before Adah, but on this day, her apology and acceptance meant more than a sack brimming with rubies.

Stifling a chuckle, Judith said, "I am not deaf to the talk on the street, but before I forget, let me see to your drink. The slander will all be forgotten when this wall is finished." Judith hurried out the door, insisting she would return with a cool cup of water.

Adah's stomach grumbled for more food. Tearing off a bigger morsel of bread, she stuffed her mouth full. Footsteps caused her to cover her mouth and force a swallow. "That was fast." She turned to find her father standing in the doorway.

Stunned, she stepped away from her food and stood, shoulders back, spine straight. A strange tingle rippled across her skin and had her wishing there was a means of escape from this crowded space. Her father hadn't entered her storeroom in…she couldn't remember the last time.

"Father, I was expecting Judith."

"So she said." Her father set a cup next to the bread basket. "I thought you would be curious about what Nehemiah had to say to the leaders of our city today. After all, you did bring a charge against us."

Adah shuffled her feet and almost tripped over her sitting stool. She braced herself against the table. "I had no choice. I had to speak for my friend and my neighbor." A rhythmic pulse battered her temples and threatened to flood her eyes as she remembered her parting with Othniel. But she would not sob like a forlorn girl. She stood in the truth of her actions. Her cheek ached as if it remembered the sting of her father's slap. "And I would do it again."

Her father laced his fingers. "You could have come to me with your concern. In private. I would have listened to your complaint. I have heard the protests of the hungry and the poor."

Her heart cinched, for she knew her father to be fair and just. "I should have." She traced a stain on her work table trying to remember if a Tonka bean or a berry had made the mark. "But I was overcome with guilt. And if I speak in truth, guilt nagged at me."

"Guilt?" Her father stepped closer. "You have labored like a slave on the wall."

The image of her father faded as tears filled her eyes. "It's not about the rocks. Or my vow to build." She swallowed and rallied the strength to bring forth a confession. "How many times did I see Beulah in the streets forlorn over her daughter's absence? I offered prayer but nothing else. I knew the landowners were struggling. I heard their outcries on the road from the city and remained silent." She rubbed her arm, but no comfort took root. Revealing her transgressions lifted her burden, briefly, but in truth, others still suffered. "I did nothing to help the people who needed it most until Othniel was allotted the same fate. Sold to work for a pagan to pay a tax." Her swallow pained her throat, for her last words were the most bitter.

Her father pressed his hands together and supported his chin with his fingertips. "Oh daughter, you are not the only one who has cast a blind eye. I did not look at our people as God sees them. I thought myself above those I was called to serve. I should have acted sooner to end the hardship in the city." He closed his eyes, but a tear escaped before his eyelids shut. "When did I lose the heart of God?"

"Never." A yearning, deep and powerful as the Great Sea, filled Adah's soul. She longed to embrace her father and kiss the tears away, but she was unclean. "We did not lose it. Oh father, we let worries make us forget God's goodness. We have battled a drought and mother's illness." She inched closer and leaned forward, feeling the exhales of her father's breath. "We relied too much on ourselves. I labored in the sun and toted a sword, but God doesn't need me to build His wall. There are many men to do His work."

"I need you, Adah." It was only a whisper, but to Adah it was an affirmation shouted in an assembly. Her father met her gaze with eyes as bright as fine-cut amber. "I will take a sword-wielding daughter over any of the sons of Judah."

Selah! The threads of Adah's muscles nearly unwound, threatening to leave her crumpled on the floor of her storeroom. "Then I will wield that sword for the household of Shallum and for the Lord, so Jerusalem will have her wall."

"You took a vow." Her father brushed the wetness from his cheeks.

"I did. And I will honor it as you have taught me." Pride swelled within her at her father's wise, honest, and apologetic words. She hadn't questioned his authority in seventeen years, and after this night, she didn't believe she would ever need to again.

Her father sniffled. "Our governor needs workers as loyal to him as you have been. Tobiah and Sanballat have influence inside our city. Even some of our priests question Nehemiah's leadership." He kissed the palm of his hand and held it before her. "Rest six more days, and then you must get back to building the wall."

Holding up her hand, Adah received the offering of his love and forgiveness without their skin ever touching. It must have been her imagination, but at that moment of reunion, the starlight streaming through her jut-rimmed window grew brighter than a silversmith's fire.

24

Adah presented her offering to the priest at the temple and was now clean and able to fulfill her vow to rebuild Jerusalem's wall. As she returned from the temple, she peeked down every lane that led to the wall and rejoiced at the progress of her people. Even at the first light of morning, her city was awake and at work. The shouting, grunting, and hammering of the builders echoed against the stone dwellings lining the streets. What a beautiful song of Judah.

First, she would check on Telem and see for herself how his wound was healing. Jehu and Jehuliel had come each day to visit their mason and report on the height of her father's section. The brothers waved when they caught sight of her longing stares from the threshold of her storeroom.

Staying away had been difficult, but she did not want to stumble or foolishly touch one of her friends, rendering them useless for a day. Every laborer was needed to reach Nehemiah's vision of a fortified city with solid gates. A vision received from the God of Abraham, Isaac, and Jacob. A vision from her God.

She burst through the door of her home. Her heart pounded against her ribs as she expected to see Telem sprawled on a mat in the living room and Judith camped at his side, but no one greeted her arrival. The room was empty of bedding and bodies. Her mother's carved oak chair waited for its owner.

"Where is my family?" she asked a servant.

Bowing, the elderly woman said, "They went to the wall, Mistress."

Adah raced out the door and down the street, rounding the crumbling corner in haste. Her throat burned with every breath.

She halted at the sight of her family. Her father, dressed in the plain tunic and turban of a laborer, shifted stone with Jehu. Her mother sat by the water jars dressed in an indigo gown as dark as the finest sapphire. Hand on her hip, Judith stirred the pitch pot. An invigorating scent of freshly cut pine tickled Adah's nostrils.

Bowing her head, Adah whispered a prayer of praise to God. Her chest cinched tight as she recounted the faithfulness of her family.

"You're late." Telem sat near a pile of cut stone and issued orders to Jehuliel.

Adah scowled at her mason. "And you should be in bed. There is no shame in healing. A sword tried to take your life."

"I have said the same thing." Judith pounded the stirring stick for emphasis. "He is as stubborn as you about finishing the wall."

Adah strode toward her sister and gave her a kiss. Queen Damaspia's fragrance mingled with the scent of sap. Did her sister wish to impress Telem? Judith could entice him with vinegar. "We are honoring a vow."

"Do you need my cloak?" Jehu's smirk tempted Adah to say yes.

"It seems I have no need of it." She scanned the progress along the wall. More men moved rock. More men made mortar. More men of Judah had heeded Nehemiah's call since the attack. "The gap I guarded has been raised and no holes remain. I do not wish my father to receive another tongue lashing from a priest if I stray from our section."

"I pray it was my last rebuke." A welcome humor hung in her father's words. Oh how her heart delighted that a man of her father's status labored among his people. "Your mother has charge of your sword."

Others might esteem her father's position and status, but to Adah, her mother's strength rivaled that of a seasoned warrior. And Adah had no doubt her mother could wield a sword better than most. Her mother heard sounds and whispers the sighted did not. After a single cricket chirp, her mother could rid the house of the pesky intruder.

"Come, and greet me daughter." Her mother held out her arms toward Adah's voice. "Izhar placed your blade behind the water jars. I pray we don't have need of it this morn."

Joining her mother in the shade, Adah put a hand on her shoulder before placing a kiss on her cheek.

Elisheba squeezed Adah's hand. "I don't know what you said to your father, but he has visited households all over the district. And when he is home, he does not leave my side." Her mother glowed like a newly betrothed girl.

Adah pressed her lips together and tried to stop the swell of pride from bursting forth in a loud song or a spirited dance. She had always respected her father, but his repentance and renewed sense of duty swelled her heart. "Father and I listened to God. *Adonai* reminded us both of why we are shifting rocks." She straightened the fray of her mother's veil. "I truly believe only God could turn a pagan king's favor toward Nehemiah. This city must be protected from those who wish to destroy it."

"Who is minding the donkey?" Telem shouted, scraping his blade over a rock. "If the beast wanders off, we will lose him to a tired Levite."

Her mother's head jerked upwards. "What is that noise?"

Did her mother hear the donkey? Standing by her side, Adah whispered, "Telem is shaving a corner one-armed. He must be feeling stronger as he's ranting again." She glanced over at her twin sister. "Judith is churning the pitch."

"It's a woman's voice." Her mother's brow furrowed. She shifted her head covering from her ear and faced east. "Can't you hear it?"

On tiptoe, Adah strained to see if a disgruntled wife chastised her husband. She didn't see a woman, but with the wall growing taller and buildings all around, people were easily hidden. She did see Nehemiah approaching on horseback. His mount bore the vibrant scarlet of the Persian king, but no cavalry rode with the governor.

"Nehemiah is coming toward us," she called out to her father and their workers. Caressing her mother's arm so as not to leave her isolated in her darkened world, Adah said, "Our governor is coming on horseback with no escort."

"Your father says he's been inspecting the wall at all hours." Her mother grimaced. "I still hear something. Is someone hurt?"

Adah shaded her face from the sun. "Judith, do you hear a voice?"

"Around here there is always noise." With a nod of her head, Judith indicated where Telem sat. She stopped stirring and searched the sky. "A bird?"

Telem glanced up. "If we are talking, we are not laboring."

As Adah took a few strides to meet the governor, he turned his horse sideways, and guided his mount toward the newly laid stones. A woman came into view. Wrapped in purple and banded with enough gold to tempt the pious, she stood with her arms outstretched toward a wisp of cloud and wailed.

Adah returned to her mother. "Forgive me, Mother, but there is a woman. She is a sight to behold wearing a purple veil and stomping the ground. I believe she is singing a lament."

"Young or old?" Her mother was on her feet, head up, and expression stern.

"Older." Adah said.

Her father abandoned Jehu's side and sprinted toward his wife.

Royally clad, the mysterious woman dashed in Adah's direction. "Repent of your traitorous ways. Repent or be slain!"

Adah's mind flashed to the temple. She had made her offering to be clean. Why was this stranger casting insults at her? Her muscles tensed. Did one of the men in the battle at the gate die? Did this woman blame her for his death?

Nehemiah maneuvered his horse to block the woman's advance. "Go home Noadiah. Stop harassing me. May God punish you for your lies."

Noadiah? The prophetess? Adah had never met the favored woman of God, but this woman had to be a fraud, for her tongue couldn't speak for God and at the same time spew curses at His people.

Dodging around the governor's mount, Noadiah

charged forward. "Stop building," she screamed. "Or your blood will fill this city."

Heat flushed Adah's cheeks. Why was the prophetess of God challenging the governor? This wall benefited God's people.

Adah kept her sandals planted firmly in the dirt. She had already faced worse insults than these.

Her father grabbed her arm and shoved her toward the crumbling corner. "Take your mother home." His stance threatened a confrontation with the prophetess.

Nehemiah leapt from his horse and joined her father.

Stepping back, Adah reached for her mother's hand.

"I am not leaving." Her mother's body went rigid. "Woe to the woman who curses my family."

The prophetess swung her arms as though warding off a dust storm and fixed her gaze on the surrounding workers. "Nehemiah brings the king's army to our gates. If you build this wall, you will die for treason." Noadiah circled around the governor and his ruler. "Nehemiah wishes to be king. He is a traitor who has seduced the city officials to follow him in a revolt."

With the pitch pot as its center, a crowd began to gather. If the people believed the prophetess's claims, would they grow violent toward the governor? Her father?

O Lord, calm all of our hearts.

"Repent," the prophetess shouted. "Your governor has deceived you. He desires to be king of Judah. War will come to your families."

"This is nonsense," Nehemiah said. "Jerusalem is

my home and the home of my fathers. I would not bring ruin upon her."

"Lies!" Noadiah hissed. "You have already brought warriors to this city. The loyal governors of Samaria and Ammon are ready for battle."

Loyal? Hah! Sanballat and Tobiah were not loyal to the One True God.

Taunts continued from the prophetess.

Adah's temper flared. Her father did not need a riot in the city. And why was a prophetess insulting Nehemiah? She had seen the governor's grief over the rubble heap Jerusalem had become after many a siege. He had been called by God to restore the glory of the city. She had believed Nehemiah the night he told her of his plans, and she believed him still. God had blessed Jerusalem through Nehemiah's courage. Someone had to disperse the crowd, lest a laborer believe the prophetess and hurl a stone at the governor.

A curious man almost tripped over her mother as he drew closer to hear the prophetess's charges. Hot, surging contempt swept through Adah's body.

Be strong and courageous and do God's work.

God had not forsaken His people. He'd sent Nehemiah to rebuild the city of David. Surely, the prophetess knew of God's plans. If she didn't, she would hear of them now.

Whirling around, Adah bent and reached for her sword. Her fingers wrapped around the hilt, but instead of withdrawing her blade, she stilled. Images of Telem's wounded body and the bloodshed at the gate, tempered her rage. How could she call her people to reason? What had Moses used to show his authority? *A stick.*

Adah did not need a staff that budded or turned into a snake, she needed something to draw attention to her defense of Nehemiah. She glanced over at the pitch pot. Judith held the stirring stick. After returning her sword to its hiding place, Adah darted toward her sister and grabbed the long pole of worn wood. "May I use this?"

Judith let go without complaint or question.

Scraping the thick pitch from the wood, Adah secured her grip on the stick. She raised her plain staff into the air and strode, fierce with purpose, toward the prophetess and Nehemiah.

Noadiah screamed and drew back, hunched like a misbehaving child waiting for discipline. Was the woman hoping for sympathy by crouching like the innocent?

Laborers retreated from their positions near the arguing.

Adah's father's eyes grew round as plums. Only the governor held his position, calm-faced and clasped-handed.

Striking the ground with the tip of her stick, Adah drew a line in the dirt deep enough to darken the earth. Then, she lifted her makeshift staff. "I, Adah *bat* Shallum made a vow to build this wall; to restore the city of our forefather David." Her voice rose as the crowd grew silent. She brandished her stick like a sword and pointed it at Noadiah. "Rantings from this woman will not stop my work or the work of my family. Would King David tear down this wall?"

A few laborers muttered their allegiance to David.

Turning, and with her stick challenging those who stood closest, she said, "Does God want us to tear down this wall?" The strength of her words strained her voice.

"No!" Laborers erupted in a defiant chant. Some lifted rocks in the air as they shouted support of their governor.

"We will do the work," her mother called out.

"You are not a prophetess." Noadiah spat at Adah's sandals.

"I am today. For I am following our governor, the man King Artaxerxes sent to rebuild our city." She thrust her staff into the air like a battle charge. "And I will fight for the man sent by our God."

"So will we," the brothers said in unison. Jehu whipped a chisel above his head as if it were a cloth.

Telem stomped his feet and marched to the pitch pot. "As will I." He positioned himself by Judith's side.

Calls of affirmation drowned out Noadiah's curses.

"That's my daughter," her mother bellowed. "My strong and courageous daughter." Her mother drummed a beat on the nearest water jug.

The prophetess clawed her hands and chastised those closest to her. "Destruction is coming. King Artaxerxes will punish you and your children." She glared at Nehemiah. "Your death awaits. The king's army will come and destroy you. Not one of your newly laid rocks will be left standing. These rocks will crush your bones."

"Leave us." Her father flicked his hand, dismissing the stunned prophetess. "Go back to Bethel and continue conspiring with Sanballat. The governor of Samaria may wish to see the destruction of Jerusalem, but our governor does not. From this day forth, you are not welcome in Jerusalem unless you bring an offering for this sin to the temple."

"Curse you Shallum. And your daughter." Noadiah squinted her pronouncement. "God will punish you for silencing His servant."

Adah leveled her staff at the men standing near the prophetess. "God's servants are all around you, prophetess. They carry their mallets and chisels and have dust on their skin. They are the *true* servants of our God."

"And some," Nehemiah said, stationing himself by Adah's side, "do the work of God with a stick."

"Woe to all who listen to your falsehoods." Noadiah jeered and shoved anyone bold enough to block her path toward the Valley Gate.

"May God remember this slander of His servant," Nehemiah called. "I am foremost and humbly the servant of God. He has made me your servant."

Adah beheld the wooden staff in her hand. The smooth tool was not as lethal as a sword. It did not pierce, impale, or kill, but today the stick had the power to end a war of words with the prophetess, and the wood didn't even have to bloom or slither. Adah trusted in the unspoken promise of protection that God had given her governor. But Noadiah was a woman of standing in Judah, and during her withdrawal she left a wake of accusations and threats. Mostly against the household of Shallum.

Be strong and courageous and do God's work.

Adah wished she could recite God's challenge without her stick trembling, but then she had never defied a prophetess before.

25

Later that afternoon, Adah hurried to her storeroom to prepare a salve for Telem's wound. Her fists balled tight any time she remembered Noadiah's slander of Nehemiah. Enemies grew more numerous by the day. Enemies of her God and of her people. Why did God allow this opposition? She sighed as she dodged slow-moving city dwellers. Maneuvering around a woman, she accidentally bumped her arm.

"Forgive me," Adah said with a quick half-turn.

"Adah?" A woman spoke her name with breathy elation.

How long had it been since someone had called out to her with such enthusiasm, happy to be in her presence? This day she would answer anyone who did not assault her with curses. Adah stopped and turned around.

Beulah's daughter stood before her, thinner than Adah remembered, clutching a small satchel under one arm.

"Leah. You're back." Adah wrapped her arms around the girl. The drape of Leah's tunic gave way under the force of Adah's embrace.

"Yes, and before my mother gives birth." Leah held onto Adah. "Your father lowered our taxes and refunded the difference for the last few months. The sum was enough to pay the merchant I served."

Consumed with pride at her father's generosity,

Adah felt as though she had grown a foot. She stepped back, untangling herself from Leah's arms and the overstuffed satchel that could rival a boulder for weight. Oh, if only Othniel would return and call to her from the street. "I am glad you are here. Your mother must be unaware of your arrival, for the neighborhood is peaceful."

"She hasn't seen me." Leah straightened her head covering. Tears glistened in the young girl's eyes. "We will always be grateful to the household of Shallum for the mercy you have shown us. I am blessed to be home with my family."

If only they had shown their mercy sooner. "Be grateful to God." Adah clasped Leah's calloused hands. "He has not forsaken us or our city."

Leah nodded. "I will. I almost did not recognize my own city. The wall has grown so tall."

"On most of our backs." Adah smiled at her truth. "Go now and surprise your mother. *Shalom* my friend."

"*Shalom*." Leah's lips quivered as she hurried off.

Watching the girl return to her birthplace, Adah's chest ached as if a thistle had burrowed into her heart. Why couldn't Othniel have lived in the district overseen by her father? She glanced down the street hoping Othniel's jovial swagger and exuberant face would come into view. It didn't. Mercy didn't reign in Rephaiah's heart. Not that she had witnessed anyway.

Adah continued on toward her workshop. She would mix a bit of lavender oil and hyssop and prevent the hint of an infection from her mason's wound. Deep in reflection, she opened the door to her storeroom. Sprigs of myrtle lay unbundled on her table. The leaves needed to be stacked before she began pouring oils. She hurried toward a cupboard for thread.

Coughs rasped from the corner of her storeroom.

Adah whipped round as a chill spiked through her body.

She was not alone.

26

"Governor!" Adah flattened a hand to her breast. Her heart felt as though it would fly across the room. She grasped her work table and willed her knees to hold her steady. "What are you doing in here?"

"Forgive me for startling you." Nehemiah strolled closer.

The boom of Adah's heart quaked her robe. She rolled her shoulders back and stepped away from her table, testing her knees to see if they were steadfast. How could she blame the governor for waiting in her storeroom after the public berating he received from the prophetess? Adah liked hiding in this room with its sweet, musty smells.

Nehemiah halted a few feet from her and rocked on his sandals. "I have something that belongs to you, and your mother told me I would find you here. I expected you'd arrive before me."

"I was delayed." She swallowed the lump lodged in her throat. "A neighbor's daughter has returned from her servitude. My father lowered their taxes and refunded the overpayment. We greeted each other in the street." She pointed in the direction of the corner where she and Leah had embraced as if the governor of Judah needed to know the exact location.

"Ah." Nehemiah grinned. "I dream about seeing our people fill this city once again."

"You would think our prophetess would have the

same dream."

She offered Nehemiah a stool. He refused.

Nehemiah picked up a clove from a bowl and rolled it between his fingertips. "One prepares for opposition from enemies, but not from one's own ranks. I do not know Noadiah's reasoning for trying to intimidate me, but I have asked our God to remember her taunts." Holding the clove to his nose, the governor closed his eyes, breathed deep, and savored the bold scent. With his constant inspection of the progress on the wall, the man must have relished an aroma that would keep him awake.

"I am surprised she did not bring Sanballat. He is quick to accuse us of wrongdoing." Adah shifted a pile of rags away from Nehemiah's ornate robe. "They're two piglets from the same sow."

Raising an eyebrow, Nehemiah laughed. "Oh, how good it is to talk with someone who is forthright."

She half-smiled at his amusement and snatched her own clove from the bowl. "I worry about another attack."

"I doubt a fellow governor would lay siege to Jerusalem without a royal decree. I have too many faithful servants who would bear arms and fight for this city." Nehemiah nodded in her direction. "Sanballat and his conspirators fear King Artaxerxes more than they fear God. I was the king's cupbearer and one of his favorite officials. His letters gave me safe conduct to Jerusalem and the timber to restore my city." He surveyed the jars near his arm and set one back with the others. "If Sanballat and Tobiah harm me for their gain, they will need to answer to the king."

"And to our God." She wrapped her arms around her waist and tried not to think of death and bloodshed.

"Oh, daughter of Shallum, if only old oaths and allegiances were easily broken like a twig."

Hadn't Telem warned her and Othniel about this same thing? How certain officials and nobles made vows to foreign leaders upon the intermarriage of their children. They thought Telem misspoke. It appeared her mason knew more than she did about such oaths.

Nehemiah removed a small pouch from his belt. "Which reminds me of the reason I am here?" He loosened the drawstring and held the small bag in one hand. "The household of Shallum has been a great ally of mine."

Did he wish to pay her for her loyalty? She readied a refusal.

The governor shook the pouch and a beaded necklace cascaded into his other hand. Her necklace, but different. He held it up as if displaying the piece in the marketplace. "I found your beads by the gate."

Adah's mouth gaped. She reached out, took the necklace, and counted the sandalwood and chrysolite beads. Four on one side. Four on the other. But in the middle shimmered an exquisite greenish-blue stone.

She fingered the unusual gem. "This cannot be mine. My chain was not silver and I have never seen a jewel this color."

"That stone belonged to my father. It is rumored to have been a gift from King Solomon to a loyal ancestor. The silver...well, I have been gifted several chains and do not care to wear them all."

Tears threatened to flood her face. "Oh, Governor. How can I thank you? My mother gave me these beads after I made a perfume worthy of a sale." Her cheeks warmed like a bread stone forgotten in the oven. "I thought they were lost or stolen. But this jewel." She fingered the blue-green gem. "How can I accept this treasure from your family?"

"If only I had more to give you." He sighed and beheld her as if she were as unique and beautiful as the gemstone. "You comforted me that night I wept in the dark, and you guarded my secret until the assembly. You have worked to restore the wall with more vigor than half the men of this city." He flailed his arms as though he argued in court. "Even today you defended my honor before a prophetess. I should have prayed for an army of Adahs."

Smiling under the light of his praise, she said, "Then we would be days behind schedule."

Even though his face was etched with lines of weariness, the governor laughed.

She beamed with delight. "God will see that we complete the wall."

Nehemiah rapped his knuckles on the table. "I believe this to be true. We will finish His work." He gathered his robe and strode toward the threshold. Turning, he said, "If there is anything you have need of, come and seek me. I will not turn you away. Your loyalty has refreshed my soul, young woman."

"As you have refreshed mine. Thank you for this gift." She clutched the necklace to her breast. *"Toda raba."*

Her mind raced. Should she ask Nehemiah to lower the taxes on Othniel's land even though it would insult Rephaiah? To what avail? Othniel chose to honor his father as she had chosen to honor hers. He would not return until his family's debts were paid. If he learned of her boldness, would he reject her? Hold a grudge?

Too late. Gone was the governor. Gone was her chance to beg for the one she loved.

Glancing at the ceiling, she prayed, "Lord, if we finish this wall, will you send the rain? Our farmers are starving."

Silence.

She removed the jar of lavender oil from the second shelf in her cupboard and breathed in the soothing scent. No matter how many sniffs she took, her heart still longed for a boy laboring in Kadesh-Barnea.

Send the rain, Lord. And please return my Othniel.

Silence.

27

The twenty-fifth day of Elul

"The Lord deserves to be praised," her father said. "We have rebuilt the ruins. Once the doors are reinforced, the gates can be shut, and we will be a fortress."

They stood where they had labored for fifty-two days. They stood as a family of laborers with Telem and the brothers joining her family for afternoon prayer. Adah, her mother, and Judith had prayed with the women, rejoicing that Jerusalem would be the grand city of Judah once more.

In all her rejoicing, Adah did not forget those still suffering in servitude, for a very round Beulah and her daughter walking arm and arm down the street were a constant reminder. If only Othniel were by her side, filled to the brim with pride at what his hands had accomplished.

She admired the fit of the stones, the color, the height. No more could she glimpse low-lying bushes and trees. Did King David touch one of these rocks? When the Babylonians attacked the city and destroyed the wall, did someone take their last breath under one of these boulders? Her people had suffered, were suffering, but now, just maybe, God was giving them a new beginning.

Telem crossed his arms without a flinch. "Our

section is the best."

Truly. "I can't believe you made me dust it with a rag."

Judith bumped her shoulder. "I think it was a jest, but you did it anyway. You do like orders."

Adah pursed her lips at her sister while the brothers laughed. "I like order not orders." She cast a glance at Telem. And yes, she had already counted the stones in their section.

Her mother tilted her face towards the sky. "It is too bad Othniel isn't here to see this. I never heard a complaint from his lips."

Agreement came from the small gathering.

"Mm-hm." Adah's composure crumbled. She rested her cheek on her mother's shoulder and clasped her mother's hand. Today was a day to celebrate. Adah had fulfilled her vow to her father and to her God. Her entire family had faithfully served the One True God. Her heart should have been pressed down with pride, but a piece of it remained with the man who had never doubted her courage.

Her father's name rang out from one of the alleys.

"Shallum." The frantic call grew louder.

Adah blew out a frustrated breath. Couldn't her father have a rest from his duties?

Her father faced the abandoned dwelling with the crumbling corner, his expression as undone as the pile of rubble.

A young man slid to a stop before her father.

"Sir, you must come at once. The prophetess has returned with an army."

Adah gasped.

Her mother trembled beneath Adah's hold.

Her father stumbled in his attempt to follow the

messenger.

The young man steadied her father's arm. "You must bring your daughter as well. Rephaiah ordered it be so."

Adah shivered, growing colder with every dark thought. Telem's wall of perfectly fitted rocks caught her sight. Would the abandoned stones be used against her? Did the officials blame her for this show of force? And for the return of the prophetess?

Tears welled in her mother's eyes.

"You can't go," Judith stammered. "It is a trick."

Telem offered her sister a drink from a waterskin. His stare, normally condescending or challenging, was as stoic as a glazed jar in her cupboard.

She shook her head. "God will not forsake me or father. We did His work." Nestling close to her mother's ear, she whispered, "Do not fret. Judith will be by your side."

With a glance toward Judith's stricken face, Adah followed after the messenger and her father, and left behind her family, friends, and fellow laborers.

Telem and the brothers headed after her, blades strapped to their belts.

She fumbled the beads on her restored necklace, stroking the stone the governor had given her as a gift.

Help me Lord.

28

A crowd of people, mostly men, amassed as if court was being held by the Fish Gate. The messenger plowed through those gathered, clearing a path and not caring if he shoved or insulted those in his way. She followed her father and prayed his status would protect her from harm. Craning her neck to see over turbans and head dressings, she spied a tribunal waiting near the doorless gate.

Four officials hovered to the left of the newly restored frame. Nehemiah was flanked by Ezra the priest and her father's counterpart, Rephaiah. At least Rephaiah's ever-haughty son Gershom was nowhere in sight. Adah's jaw clenched at Rephaiah's stern-faced stare. No doubt her summons suited his attempt to have his son replace her father as ruler of a half-district of Jerusalem.

Five priests stood on the right of the city's entrance, including her foe, Delaiah, who had refused to blow the shofar to save his own people. It was strange, but her accuser wore a brightly dyed purple head band.

Lord, I've done the work. Please do not forsake me.

"There she is," a man bellowed. "She's the girl who insulted the prophetess."

Someone's spit dampened her chin. She wiped the wetness on her robe and hastened to catch her father.

"The daughter of Shallum is the false prophetess,"

a laborer yelled.

Worse indignations flooded the gathering space.

Sweat dripped down the side of her face while a sea of perspiration pooled above her lip. "God of Jacob, I need to be brave."

"The witch is prophesying." Her first greeter offered another taunt. Why couldn't the man stay silent?

Rephaiah met her father before they reached the circle of officials. Arms crossed and legs in a wide-stance, he acted like he was the judge at this tribunal. "Did I not instruct you to discipline your daughter, Shallum? Her tirade against Noadiah has soldiers camped at our gate. Sanballat has brought over eight-hundred men from Samaria to savor our undoing."

Several men nodded in agreement.

"Ah, my friend." Her father opened his arms as if to hug his fellow ruler. "Is my daughter so powerful that a rebuke from her lips puts our city in peril?"

A laugh roared behind her. She turned to find Telem and the brothers listening to the conversation.

Toda raba, Adonai.

"She is an untamed fool." Rephaiah retorted. "Perhaps this time the governor will see her sinful ways."

Adah hid her fisted hands in the folds of her robe. Throwing her shoulders back, she held Rephaiah's slit-eyed condemnation without a flinch, although every measure of her body flamed hotter than a torch. She pressed her lips together and did not answer the ruler's insult.

"Do you have need of me, Rephaiah?" Nehemiah stood a few feet beyond the chattering ruler. "I believe we are conferring by the gate."

Rephaiah acknowledged the governor with a slight nod. "Yes, all the better for the girl to see our enemies lying in wait for a battle."

Her father shook his head. "Why should they want to do battle now when our walls are restored and Tobiah is not seated at Sanballat's side? Tobiah delighted in burning our fields and speaking ill of our God."

"Because." Telem stepped from her shadow. "If Nehemiah is accused of treason, Sanballat could petition the king to govern this neighboring land and control the trade that goes with it." Telem cast a glance in her direction. "I was not deaf in the caves. Jerusalem is becoming a prized jewel." Telem announced his proclamation to those who stood listening nearby. "A thief like Sanballat will devise a way to snatch it from our people."

The brothers agreed and started a raucous among those who heard her mason.

"Why is this laborer allowed to speak?" Rephaiah huffed.

"He is a Levite." Ezra paraded over from the gate toward Rephaiah and castigated anyone who did not disperse to let him pass. "I knew this mason's father. Hasn't he been working for Shallum?"

"A son would not be dearer to me." Her father clapped Telem on the back.

Telem looked as shocked as she felt. But she would grasp any support that was given.

"Woe that you did not have a son, Shallum." Rephaiah *tsked* at her, sounding as though he had food stuck in his teeth.

Adah breathed deep, her chest plumping like a bothered hen. Enough of this banter. If armies waited to do battle, then why was no one lined up for war? "Why was I summoned if I am not a son? There are plenty of officials here to ride out and meet this envoy."

Nehemiah bowed his head and pressed his hands together. "Sanballat and Tobiah have been sending messengers for a while. Their letters are all the same, asking me to meet them at a location outside of this city. I have never agreed to their requests. A message from Artaxerxes is different. I must receive it and answer the king. It is my duty."

Telem raked a hand through his hair. "Can't they bring it into the city?"

"They won't," Rephaiah snapped. "The daughter of Shallum scolded the prophetess. It is no wonder they believe this is a trap, and we will revolt and kill any messengers. Some nobles believe the prophetess. They believe her claim of treason to be true. Noadiah is well respected among the people."

She heard his unspoken inference—and you are not. *Be strong and courageous and do God's work. God will not forsake us.*

Adah cleared her throat and then asked, "If they desire to talk with the governor, why am I here?" Her defiant gaze moved from her father to Rephaiah to Ezra and then to Nehemiah.

"The king summoned you as well," Nehemiah answered. "No doubt Sanballat and the prophetess have slandered your name. By including you in their schemes, they cast doubt on your father's loyalty."

And it would be easier to kill a woman than a respected ruler. *Oh Lord, protect my family. I meant to bring my father honor, not shame.*

Shielding her eyes with her hand, she observed

Nehemiah's face for any sign of worry. He did not act or look downcast like he did the night she found him weeping for his forefathers and his city. He did not tremble or tear his embroidered robes. His calmness soothed the terror of his people. And it soothed her.

"My daughter cannot go." Her father's body teetered. "If they think she is planning treason against the king, they will kill her on the spot in front of this city. As a warning."

"What is one girl?" Rephaiah's breathy comment settled in her ears.

Swallowing as if this were the last bite of her final meal, Adah said, "I will go." She stepped closer to Nehemiah. "I was one of the first people to hear of the governor's plan to rebuild Jerusalem. If my life has to end, it will end with the governor at my side, and the vision of our wall in my sight. I believe God desires our city to rise from the rubble. And I will not rest until the gates are secure and Jerusalem is strong."

"This is the City of David." Telem shouted. "The men of Judah will defend it."

Bystanders agreed.

Rephaiah pushed some gawkers aside. "Look," he said, pointing to the outskirts while his eyes showered her with disdain. "Observe what awaits this city and its rulers."

In the distance, expanding as far as she could see outside the northern gate, down the main road, and shaded by a scattering of trees, were soldiers. She had beheld raiders from this army when Othniel's fields burned.

Crooked-nosed Sanballat perched on a mount in front of his men. Twirling and stomping in glee at his side was the purple-clad false prophetess. She frolicked as if the ground was set ablaze. The fighting men of King Artaxerxes sat atop horses decorated with the golden-yellow and pomegranate red of Persia. Breastplates, swords, and spears shone in the sun's glare.

The conspirators gave Adah no fright, but the envoy from the king ground her fortitude to flour. Men trained to kill did not bring greetings. But they were not a legion. She hastily counted fifty warriors.

Closing her eyes, she prayed aloud, "Lord, I trust You will not forsake us, and I believe that Your servant Nehemiah is doing Your work. Protect us with Your army. Show our enemies there is but One True God, the God of Abraham, Isaac, and Jacob. And that You are here with us. And me."

She stepped back and flung her arms wide, moving back and forth as if she were the prophetess of this city. Her charge to the men gripping swords and fidgeting with arrows would be one of encouragement, not despair.

"I am ready to meet our visitors," she said.

"As am I." Nehemiah whipped his arm in the air as if he stood ready to release a sling stone.

Telem squinted out toward the hills. "Not yet."

Rephaiah stomped his sandal. "We cannot keep an envoy from the king waiting. The soldiers will believe we are planning a revolt."

"And if they are planning to attack, we need to win." Telem regarded her with a smirk. "Do you not remember how King David took this city from the Jebusites?" He mimicked shoving something heavy over his head.

She smiled in remembrance of being flung out of Telem's tunnel. "Listen to my mason." Rejuvenated of spirit, she stood tall and fixed a scorned noblewoman's gaze on the officials. "He knows how to get men to the hills and trap our enemy if we have to fight. For we will fight if Sanballat charges the gate." She glanced at the men near the entrance. They wore plain tunics and carried lackluster blades. Sanballat may disregard their fortitude, but she would throw her lot in with them any day. Rotating in a tight circle, she shouted, "We will fight like men—"

"And women," Telem interjected with a nod.

"Of Jerusalem." She raised a fist toward the cloudless sky.

As her proclamation hung in the air, her father came by her side and placed a hand on her shoulder. "Let it be so," her father shouted. "God will give us the victory."

Now, no matter what happened, with her vow fulfilled to build the wall and her father's praise in front of the city's officials, she could meet whatever end God decried. With another shiver hovering just beneath her skin, she recited a prayer of King David's. "Rescue us O' Lord, from evil men and protect us from men of violence." Turning to behold all who listened, she yelled with abandon, "Be strong and courageous!"

Nehemiah echoed her charge. He and Ezra and her father added a hearty, "*Selah!*"

29

Needing to buy time and prevent a charge on the Fish Gate, Adah and Nehemiah strolled, slowly and honorably, through the gate's frame and toward the king's men and Sanballat's misguided fools.

A slight breeze brought the scent of freshly cut cedar and oak to her nostrils. Adah kept her gaze on the army before her. If she glanced toward the hills, it might reveal their plot and put her people in peril. But that didn't mean she did not think about her trip to summon Telem from his cave, or the boy who went with her. Her chest tightened recalling Othniel's bravery. At least serving pagans, he was not here to face a battle, or see her slain because of wicked lies.

"We advance toward uncertainty, possibly death," Nehemiah said. "And I cannot see one wrinkle on your face. When I came to Jerusalem I did not know if our people would agree to rebuild the wall. After meeting you that night, my heart knew God's plan would be victorious."

"I do not deserve so much praise." Her heavy footfalls lightened at the governor's encouragement, but her stomach ached as if she'd consumed pebbles with her bread. "My mother heard you weeping, and I sought out the noise to calm her fears."

"But you listened as I revealed the burden I carried, and you kept my secret."

She regarded Nehemiah. His cadence and fine

clothing revealed his status, but his heart convinced her to champion his cause.

"When we met, you told me how you prayed before approaching the king for a leave of duty and for letters for safe passage. At great risk to your own life, you spoke for this city and our people. God's people."

Nehemiah nodded.

"How could I not follow your lead when we had been petitioning God to raise Jerusalem from its rubble?"

"My heart nearly stopped when the king asked me why I was sad." Nehemiah grinned. "This heart of mine has been worked harder than an Egyptian slave." He patted his chest. "But it still beats."

"Mine too." Rapidly. She avoided assessing the strength of the army camped around her city. "I have learned more about God in the last two months than I have since birth. And I owe that knowledge to you." She beheld him with the calm of a sleeping newborn and gave her governor a reassuring smile.

"*Toda raba*, my brave Adah."

Her smile vanished. Othniel had used that same affection. Her childhood friend would want to be at her side showing these foreigners the strength and courage of their people. *So I shall.*

She glanced back at the gate and recognized her father a few paces outside of the city, watching her walk to greet heavily armed warriors. His stature seemed like a child's against the height and grandeur of the newly completed wall. A wall God had raised with the hands and backs of His people.

She prayed for God to work His peace in her trembling limbs as she and Nehemiah strolled closer to their accusers. Even a whiff of the jasmine scenting her veil did nothing to relieve her angst. "Be strong and…" Her mouth was too dry to finish her chant.

"Woe to you Nehemiah and your witch, I have escorted the king's cavalry to your city so I could witness the punishment of your treasonous acts," Sanballat called from the center of a line of men carrying swords.

Leave it to the Samaritan governor to place himself where he had the best defense.

Noadiah shook a tambourine and paraded along the station of soldiers. Gold beads swayed from her headband, but she wore the same plum-colored robe from her previous visit. Her exaggerated steps and flailing arms fanned the stench of horse sweat and unbathed fighting men in Adah's direction. "Death to those who do not heed God's wisdom."

And what god would that be? Adah's fury soared at Noadiah's false teaching. Now was the time to snuff out the lies of rebellion and impress the truth on the king's messenger.

A flash of light burst forth from the hills. The small flicker from Telem's polished bronze mirror calmed her soul.

David and his mighty fighting men had overtaken this city and had conquered the Jebusites by using tunnels, and today, if need be, Sanballat and Noadiah would be brought low by Jerusalem's underground laborers. Praise God for her mother who sent her and Judith on a mysterious journey to find a mason. And praise God for a willing escort. Her Othniel.

"Come closer." Sanballat waved Nehemiah in the direction of his mount. "You make us wait as if you have the power of a king."

"If I thought myself as lofty as you suggest, I

would be atop a stallion with a golden sword." Nehemiah veered to address the commander of the king's forces. "I walk as a servant of King Artaxerxes and the Most High God."

"Is your god mightier than mine?" Sanballat shouted.

Yes. But only a fool would answer Sanballat's question. Contempt for his fellow governor riddled every word. Adah stayed a half-pace behind Nehemiah, using his body as a shield from the scrutiny of the soldiers and from their insults.

Nehemiah halted near the leader of the king's envoy. He left enough distance to uphold his standing as the royal cupbearer, and he left enough room for a hasty escape.

"Lord, save us from these men of violence." Her whisper broadened Nehemiah's stance.

The king's official dismounted and marched toward Nehemiah. His regal breastplate held so much silver that he sparkled in the afternoon sun.

Sanballat remained on his wide-withered horse.

"Governor." The armor-clad leader gave Nehemiah a nod of respect. He handed the governor a parchment sealed with wax and embedded with the mark of the king. "Our sovereign has sent an urgent message. I am to carry out its commands."

"Artaxerxes knows of your intentions," Sanballat announced. "I am not the only governor to share concerns about this wall. Tobiah has brought forth charges. Why fortify a city if not for war?"

Tink-tat-tink. Noadiah added her slander.

Nehemiah turned toward his fellow governor. "Who would spread such rumors except those who scheme to deceive the king?"

"You cannot silence God." Noadiah rattled her tambourine all the more.

No, but could someone silence her? Adah breathed deep and slowly blew out a breath, attempting to calm the rage stoked by her enemies. Noadiah's dagger-eyed glares heaped wood on Adah's inner fire pit. With one arm around her middle and another on her necklace, Adah counted her beads and recited, "Hear, O, Israel, the, Lord, is, our, God, the, Lord, alone."

Sanballat rode forward. "Your pride has brought you to ruin."

"We will know if you are a prophet when I open the seal." Nehemiah's accommodating tone had worn thin. "You certainly have been earnest in trying to draw me out of the city, Sanballat. It is a shame you have to interfere in my personal business with the king." He stepped to the side, leaving Adah exposed to gawking fighters.

Stopping her bead count, Adah gave a nod of respect to the king's messenger and clasped her hands behind the folds of her robe.

"The daughter of Shallum has assisted me in rebuilding the wall of this fine city. She holds the king in high regard, but she holds our God in the highest regard."

Adah dipped her head in agreement with her governor.

Sanballat cleared his throat and regarded the official. "We do not blaspheme our neighbor's gods."

"Open the decree." Noadiah shook her tambourine. "He stalls his demise."

Nehemiah held the message in the air above his head.

Adah's lips were dry as linen. The pounding of her

heart bested Noadiah's raucous music.

Her precious governor slid a finger underneath the seal, opened the parchment, and slowly read the king's edict to himself. Holding the message to his chest, her governor roared with a laughter that echoed above the soldiers. The messenger's horse neighed and sidestepped toward another stallion.

"Tell us what it says." Noadiah's prophetic skills failed her.

Nehemiah bent at the waist and laughed boldly as though he had enjoyed too much wine. Tears streamed down his cheeks.

Adah rubbed her damp palms together and drew closer to Nehemiah. What had caused her governor to come undone? His belly-deep laughter stirred a rumbling among the skeptical soldiers.

"Sir, what does the king desire?" she asked.

Trying to calm his outburst, Nehemiah choked out, "You."

30

"Me!" Adah rasped. She stood with her mouth open, willing the craziness to make sense. What was Nehemiah talking about? Was this her punishment for rebuking the prophetess and encouraging the finishing of the wall? Was she to become a concubine to a foreign king? Did Artaxerxes believe her father had enough influence over their people that a marriage to her would prevent a riot?

"I have never met our sovereign." Her words came out with indignation.

The commander gave her a stern perusal.

"But it would be an honor." She would say anything to keep her city and her people safe.

"You misunderstand me." Nehemiah reigned in his giddiness. "There is no need for you to see the king."

She jerked backward. Did the king want to put her away in his harem? Bits of light blurred her vision. Her skin chilled under the relentless sun. Jerusalem was her home. Jerusalem was Othniel's home. Jerusalem was where he would expect her to be waiting. "Am I to leave Judah?"

Noadiah pranced, kicking up dust. "I am vindicated. Her lawlessness will not be tolerated here or in Susa."

"Be still," Nehemiah snapped. "The daughter of Shallum is not going anywhere."

Praise the Lord! She shuffled her feet and willed her bones to keep her upright.

The prophetess scowled and hugged her tambourine.

"Adah." Nehemiah's voice softened. "It's your gift. Your perfume has delighted the queen. The king requests more of the fragrance at once."

Was this truly the reason soldiers waited outside of Jerusalem? For a fragrance? Her fingers tingled as if they had emptied of blood. This was no dream. God had not forsaken His people. People who had listened to His servant and done the hard work of restoring Jerusalem's wall.

She glanced at the official. "This is all you have need of?" Oh, if only she could dance like Noadiah and not look like a fool. "The queen will have her perfume. I will prepare it without delay."

"Nonsense." Sanballat slid off his horse and stomped toward the king's messenger. "Read the words for yourself. This is more trickery from rebel Jews. Certainly the queen has the best perfumers in Persia."

Nehemiah handed the parchment to the king's official.

The battle-ready messenger read the edict. His stature grew tall and rigid. "The governor of Judah has spoken the truth."

"Then that potion is bewitched," Noadiah said. "It's sorcery."

"What do I have to hide?" With a raise of his eyebrow and a dip of his chin, Nehemiah challenged his fellow governor. "Read the message yourself. However, the king does seem fervent in his request. Perhaps a special occasion is near?"

In the few moments of silence, Adah turned her back on the soldiers, governors, and officials, and found her father standing as tall and regal as the newly crafted Fish Gate. She crossed her hands and held them over heart. One beat. Two. Her father did the same.

As she turned back to the commotion, she sneaked a peek at the cliffs. The hills hid the army of Judah; laborers, masons, fathers, sons. No one would guess the catacombs were filled with fighting men. *Protect us from men of violence O' Lord.*

The king's official ripped the parchment from Sanballat's hands. "Our sovereign requests a perfume from the daughter of Shallum. It is as the governor of Judah says."

Sanballat rounded on Noadiah. "Where is their treason? The makings of a revolt? You almost started a war."

Noadiah's right hand became a claw threatening her cohort. "All of Samaria believes my prophecies. Nehemiah is deceiving you. I have never spoken falsely."

"Until now," Adah said.

"You." Holding her tambourine overhead, Noadiah shook it with a fury. "You are not a prophetess."

Adah retreated away from Noadiah and closer to Nehemiah, fearing the annoying instrument might come down on her scalp.

"Perhaps the Hebrew woman should be a prophetess." The official addressed Nehemiah. "I only allowed the governor and this seer to accompany my men because of their standing in Susa. I could not take the rumor of a rebellion lightly. Nor an ambush." He flashed a stern look at Sanballat. "I will proceed into the city?" His inferred order to Sanballat was that the Samaritan would not accompany him.

Nehemiah opened his arms wide and let his sleeves drape, displaying his adornments. "I would be honored to welcome you to the city of my fathers. We have made great progress with the king's favor." Nehemiah waited as the official mounted his horse. "You may report on our success when you return to the palace." He indicated for Adah to join the procession. "I'm sure the daughter of Shallum will have the queen's portion in no time." Nehemiah arched his eyebrows with expectation.

Adah swallowed hard. "Very soon." Praise be she was not greedy with her scents as Judith possessed some of the queen's fragrance. And praise be to her mother who made smelling every bloom, grass, nut, and bean in the area a blessing.

"Do make your presence known on your return visit," Sanballat called out to the king's messenger. Even though his men outnumbered the king's procession, the Samaritan's leather and bronze armor paled in comparison to the brilliance of the silver and shiny metals of the Persians. The governor of Samaria would be a fool to start a skirmish.

Adah held in a laugh. Well, he would be more of a fool.

Farewell you men of violence.

Noadiah commandeered a donkey and trotted toward the hills. Her purple veil fluttered in the wind.

Oh, if she would only come face-to-face with the warriors of Jerusalem. For that would truly be justice for her slanderous accusations.

Adah could not bask in pride about her own abilities. Jerusalem was safe for now, but to keep the king happy she had to recreate an original perfume. And fast.

31

The closer she came to the gate, the faster she moved.

Men of Judah peered from behind the frame, from rooftops, and even secretly from far off cliffs.

Praise be to the One True God that none of their blood was shed this day. Her skin warmed, not from the sun, but from the greatness of their God. *You did not forsake me.*

Spying her father, she broke out into a dignified run. She welcomed the dust, the sour odor of bodies, and the smoke from cooking fires. This was her city, Jerusalem, the City of David.

"Father," she called, her throat aching from her dash.

Her father reached out and took her hands.

"There will be no battle. The king wants more of our gift. Of my perfume."

Rephaiah coughed, making a long guttural sound. "There goes your daughter again Shallum. She speaks but does not make any sense."

Her father caressed her hand with his thumb and then released his hold. "And where is your son, Gershom?" He shielded his eyes and pretended to survey the crowd. A few by-standers chuckled. "I did not see a son of yours face the army of Artaxerxes."

"And speaking of armies." Nehemiah passed through the entrance with his arms held high. "Where are the bars for these gates? Jerusalem is not defenseless anymore."

Cheers greeted the governor's announcement.

Taking a few steps toward the rulers, Nehemiah said, "Rephaiah, don't you have sons sitting idle?"

The pious ruler balked.

"After all," Nehemiah continued, "we will need many strong backs to secure the bars. The household of Shallum will be too busy to assist. They must be in service to our king."

"Of course." Rephaiah assessed the armor of Artaxerxes' messenger. "I will summon my sons at once."

Satisfied as she was to see Rephaiah humbled, in front of laborers no less, her insides whirled as her mind listed all the duties she must perform to recreate a fragrance. But before she crumbled one bit of cassia into olive oil, she knew who she had to visit first.

"Forgive my haste in leaving." Adah bowed. Her feet itched to carry her down the straight street and through the eastern alleys. "I do not want to keep our sovereign waiting."

With one last head bob, she was off, scrambling past the temple, through the gathering space, and around curious city dwellers, to Othniel's home. Oh, how she wished he was there with his words of encouragement to calm her fears. Was this an answer to her prayer? Could she make enough perfume to please the king and have enough left to sell to purchase Othniel's freedom?

She knocked on the door as was proper. One foot tap. Two. She burst into the living room, startling a spooked Zipporah and her daughter-in-law.

"Are we at war?" the mother gasped.

"No. Praise God." Adah clutched her breast. Her heart hammered faster than Telem's mallet. "We are safe. Our enemies are gone."

"*Selah.*" Zipporah collapsed into a chair. "I have lifted petitions to God but my sons have not returned."

And one of your sons is not in the cliffs or amassed at the gate or along the wall. Adah shook off any grievance to focus on the task at hand.

"I need more jars like the one Othniel sold me." His name took root in her throat. Swallowing, she continued. "It was made of gold and pearl and came in a cedar case."

Zipporah's brow furrowed. "I used to own several of those pieces but not anymore. I cannot afford to purchase them, and no one has the means to buy such craftsmanship."

"King Artaxerxes has enough money. And he has asked me to make a special perfume for his queen." Deep down she was still convincing herself these words were not lies. "I need as many of those bottles as you can find. You will have a royal escort to wherever you need to go."

Flipping her slightly gray hair over her shoulder, Zipporah's eyes shone with a renewed fervor. She beckoned Adah to come sit in a chair next to her at the dining table. "The king sent an envoy to receive this perfume?"

"Yes. I plan to make as much as I can so the queen can share her fragrance as a gift."

Zipporah shook her head. "No woman desires others to be the same, look the same, or even smell the same. Make another scent for the queen to gift her confidants."

"Two perfumes." Adah clasped her hands. Did she

have the time?

Leaning close, Zipporah said, "Your name will be known throughout Persia. Others will come to your father's door in search of the same fragrance. You can do this. I will help you." The blaze in her brown eyes was big enough to set the room on fire. "Othniel spoke of your skill." Her voice caught. "He would be proud of this recognition."

Adah folded her arms and rested against the edge of the table. Thinking about the hardship Othniel faced while she mixed oils for the king burdened her soul. She met Zipporah's tear-filled gaze. "Is there any way he can return sooner?"

"I pray every day."

"As do I." Adah embraced the distraught mother before she rose to leave.

"Daughter." Zipporah's voice was but a wisp. "Create the best fragrances so all of Persia will delight in the fragrant rose that is Jerusalem."

"And that rose will beget many blooms. When God sends the rain." Adah bent and kissed her friend's cheek. "*Shalom.*"

She hurried to find Judith and reclaim the original mixture of perfume. Could she recreate the scent without her sister's gift? Her mother had taught her well, but a reminder would rally her confidence.

Judith paced outside their home. Had she heard about the king's request? Perhaps she even had the jar of perfume with her. *Bless you, Judith.* Adah called out to her sister.

Halting her frenzied walk, Judith looked up, face pale, eyes swollen. "He's gone," she said, her voice strained.

Her sister couldn't be referring to Othniel. He had

been gone for some time. Did Judith not realize Adah had witnessed the retreat of Sanballat and his soldiers? Her poor sister was distraught. "Who's gone?" she asked.

"Telem. He never returned from the hills."

32

Sadness shadowed her triumph. Why Telem's disappearance should bother her, she did not know. But it did. Sure they had finished the wall, but to go off without a word was a disgrace. How could her mason leave her like Othniel? Telem saw how upset she was at her friend's absence? How could he put Judith through the same grief?

She hid her displeasure and reached out to her sister. Wrapping her arms around Judith, she said, "Perhaps our Telem is delayed in his return. He may have possessions still in the cave."

Judith shook her head. "Jehu and Jehuliel waited for him. They said he vanished in the catacombs."

"You cooked for him as for a king." Adah swiped a tear from her sister's cheek. "When his stomach grumbles, he will be at our door."

"I thought he cared for me." Judith sniffed. "He spoke tender words during his recovery. He even took my hand and held it as if I were the one needing comfort."

"I know he cared," a woman said.

Adah and Judith startled.

Their mother stood in the doorway, her forehead creased, her lips thin as a blade of grass.

"Mother!" You were listening?" Judith's eyes grew wide with shock.

"I did not hear anything that I did not already know." Their mother's eyebrows arched. "Except the hand holding." Their mother sighed. "Maybe it's time I spoke of the past. Telem is not here to share his troubles." She motioned to Adah and Judith. "You girls, come inside."

Was her mother going to break her silence and reveal a long-held truth? Did it mean Telem might never return? Her stomach sank with the heaviness of a millstone. Poor Judith. Her sister had grown even fonder of Telem than Adah had suspected.

Adah placed a hand on Judith's back and accompanied her inside the house.

Judith balked. "I should not have bothered you. You have oils to mix for the king."

"The king can wait." Adah would not miss this revelation she and Othniel had whispered about for so long. She grasped her sister's hand. "You and I traipsed through a cave to find that man. You deserve to hear about his past and his reasons for leaving." Adah kissed her sister's forehead. "Besides, you need not worry about my work, for you have some of the queen's perfume. Now we will finally hear about the man who has taken hold of your heart."

Judith squeezed Adah's hand. "See, it is not a bad idea to be bold and share one's feelings."

"No, it's not." Adah's heart pinched. Speaking boldly had not brought Othniel back to her. *Watch over him and Telem, Lord.*

Adah settled her mother into the high-backed chair in the corner. Judith lounged on a pillow next to their mother while Adah sat on the other side of the chair. Vibrant scarlet threads in the pillow's tapestry on which she sat, reminded Adah of Persia's colors and of how stark Zipporah's house had become since the rain refused to fall.

Their mother sighed. "I am not a gossip, but considering how close you have worked with Telem, and his obvious regard for you, my daughters, I will share my thoughts on why he might have left."

"To see his wife?" Judith shifted closer to the armrest as if the question was foremost in her thoughts.

"No. Of that I am certain." Her mother's eyes blinked as if she envisioned a memory. "Telem and his father helped to rebuild our temple. Before the temple was complete, Telem's father died. His mother had already passed. Being the sole heir, and child, Telem grieved terribly." Her mother's lips pressed together. "His heart was heavy. His family was gone. He married shortly after the mourning period. Too soon, I believe, for he married a foreign-born woman who did not worship our God."

Judith sunk into her pillow. "That is forbidden."

Adah tried not to judge her mason. Hadn't neighbors slandered her actions with no understanding of her reasons? "Why did the chief priest allow such lawlessness?"

Gazing across the room, her mother squinted as if the events of old played in real time in a vision. "Several priests had taken foreign wives. It became a common practice. No one protested until Ezra held them accountable to the Law." Her mother reached out, fingered Judith's head covering and stroked the cloth. "Ezra said if the priests defied God and kept their idol worshipping wives, they could not serve in God's temple. If they gave their wives up, their status and positions would remain in good standing."

"Those poor women." Judith's words were but a vapor. "Their lives would be ruined. How could they return to their fathers with no husband?"

"Did Telem send his wife away? Back to her people?" Adah's heart ached for the girl.

Her mother nodded. "I escorted his wife back home. Telem paid them in gold to receive her, and I stayed on for a while to make sure she was treated well."

Adah vaguely remembered a time when her mother's cousin came to visit. She couldn't recall why or where her mother may have traveled, but their house was oddly silent.

Judith rested her chin on her knees. "Why are you so sure he hasn't returned to his wife?"

"Telem was distraught at her departure, but I think, in time, he became more grieved at how he disobeyed God and brought dishonor on his family name." Leaning forward, her mother said, "One day, he left the city. Seasons passed, and he did not return. I believe he was angry. Mostly with himself. But also with God."

"He was not angry with me." Judith traced the dips and curves of the carved armrest with her finger. "Perhaps after a time of prayer and fasting he will return."

"He owes us that much." Annoyance emboldened Adah's words. "Telem may have come back to Jerusalem to repay a debt he owed our mother, but we saved his life. Jehu and Jehuliel treated him like a brother. His father rebuilt the temple and Telem has rebuilt the wall. This is his city. He cannot abandon it. He cannot abandon us." Adah jumped to her feet. "He won't."

With a satisfied grin crossing her face, her mother said, "That same passion I hear in your voice will bring Telem back to our city. And to our Judith. He is free to marry a daughter of Jacob and have a union blessed by God. I may not have been able to see Telem's face, but I heard the affection in his whispers."

Judith blushed at their mother's utterance.

"A troubled heart brought Nehemiah home to Jerusalem. May our friends find their way home as well." Adah prayed her beliefs would come true. Telem and Othniel had to return to Jerusalem. She wanted their presence in her life. Without them, her future would be like a bud that never fully blossomed. She kissed her mother's cheek. "Now I must use the talents you bestowed on me to create perfume for a queen."

"I will get the jar you gave me." Judith hurried toward the hall. A glimmer of hope shone through her worry.

Adah turned to her mother and stroked her hand. "Thank you, for sharing an old truth. You were a brave woman to travel to a foreign land."

Her mother stopped Adah's caress and held fast. "Let no one say the wife, and daughters of Shallum do not rise to a challenge."

Adah had one challenge left.

33

Days later, in the seventh month

"Are you coming?" Judith tapped her sandal on the floor of the storeroom. Each *thap* caused her mustard and scarlet robe to shake.

"Yes, yes. Soon." Adah secured the silver cap to her perfume bottle. Zipporah had used her best bartering skills to acquire jars overlaid with silver and gold, and set with stones. "I'm almost done with this one."

Judith sighed. "Only you would make the governor and Ezra wait."

After wiping her hands, Adah banded her linen head covering. "All of Jerusalem will be at the assembly. With women and children milling about, no one will notice we are later than most."

"What about Father?" Judith asked the question, but no lines of worry wrinkled her forehead. Her face had shown little expression since the news of Telem's abandonment. "He will be anxious for our arrival."

Adah untied her apron, set it on the table, and clasped a hand on each of Judith's shoulders. "All Father will see when we make it to the Water Gate is how beautiful you look." She kissed her sister's cheek. "Do not worry. Our mason will return." *Please, Telem. For her sake. And mine.*

Judith nodded and turned away. "Mother's

waiting."

Adah followed Judith into the street. Their mother stood outside their dwelling, eyes closed, her face basking in the sun.

"Pick up those sandals. No shuffling." Her mother held out her arms. "The trade winds will blow into the assembly before we do."

"Not today. "Adah gazed at the sky her mother could not behold. "There is not a wisp of white to block God's vision of His people."

Adah guided her mother and sister east toward the Water Gate. She didn't want to miss any of what Ezra the priest had to say, but she wanted to be ensure her mother's safety. If Jerusalem were a bouquet of flowers, its stems would be nourished by the pools near the gate.

A few women hurried by carrying their children as a mass of people gathered inside the Water Gate. Ezra positioned himself at a podium set high on a platform. The elderly priest held court in front of cedar planks that created new doors to the city. Fresh wood, a gift of the king's forests, prevented any visitor from entering Jerusalem. This day, only the people of God gathered to hear their priest.

Behind the gift of a new gate, terraced withering and burnt vineyards and fields. Adah shook the desolation from her mind and beheld the elder priest. In his place of prominence, no one could deny his authority or claim ignorance of his forthcoming message. Nehemiah, rulers, and officials flanked Ezra's sides, but the Book of the Law occupied the seat of honor, lying open and perched at the priest's waist.

Adah found some room off to the side of the platform where her mother wouldn't be jostled. With every man, woman, and child rising to their feet, or pressing forward as Ezra began to speak, the tardiness of the household of Shallum went without notice.

Ezra scanned the crowd. He raised his arms toward a vibrant blue sky that looked like it rested on top of Jerusalem's wall.

"Praise the Lord. Rejoice in His deliverance. The Lord is near." Ezra stretched out his body as if to pull the heavens into his chest. "Rejoice in His commands."

"Amen," shouted a nobleman.

"Amen," echoed the crowd.

Amen!

"God has chosen to restore the city of His servant David. He has shown His faithfulness to His people and thwarted our enemies. First with the rebuilding of His temple." Ezra gestured toward the holy place. "And now with the wall. Let us listen to his commands so we can continue in His favor."

Adah pressed her lips together. Her temples pulsed as Ezra continued to read the Law. *Bring our people back, Lord, to You and to this city.*

After Ezra's reading of God's commands, the Levites explained every word.

When Adah's heart was filled with God's promises, she dropped to her knees and worshipped the God of Abraham, Isaac, and Jacob. Packed soil warmed her skin, but she would not complain about the heat or the dust, for from the sweat and labor of her people, her city had risen. The wall was a gift bestowed by her God. A reminder of His faithfulness to His people in hard times and good times. A reminder of His faithfulness to her and her vow. *Selah, Adonai!*

Nehemiah and Ezra began to recite the *Shema*.

"Hear O Israel," Nehemiah began.

"The Lord is our God, the Lord alone." Ezra closed his eyes like he knelt by himself in an inner chamber. "Love the Lord your God, with all your heart..."

"With all your soul." Judith wept.

Adah's throat throbbed and ached as she kept in song with those kneeling beside her. "And with all your might." She squeezed her mother's hand, for Elisheba, wife of Shallum, was the mightiest woman she knew.

"Do not be filled with sorrow for your past transgressions," Nehemiah shouted over the huddled mass of people. "The joy of the Lord is our strength. Today we shall not mourn. Today we will delight in our God."

Sitting up, Adah fixed her gaze on her governor. He had petitioned the king knowing that his life might be taken from him. But God had called Nehemiah to restore the wall, and God was with Nehemiah as he spoke with Artaxerxes. And God had been with her as she fought raiders and a prophetess.

Judith's sobs cinched Adah's heart.

"Lord, Your work is not done," Adah mumbled. "The men we love are outside this wall."

"Do you hear that?" her mother asked.

Adah stood. "Yes, we are to rejoice this day."

"Listen, my daughter." Her mother fumbled for Adah's sleeve. "Do you hear it?"

Pushing the veil from her ear, Adah listened. Far off in the distance, a rumble groaned.

It can't be. Not after all this time.

Her mother sniffed the air and called out, "God is sending the rain. I can smell the dampness."

People nearby stared as if her mother were mad.

"I'm sure it will come soon." Adah smoothed a

hand down her mother's arm.

"What are you gawking at?" Judith snapped at a grim-faced woman.

Arms whipping toward the cloudless sky, her mother shrieked, "It is almost here. God's blessing."

People shuffled away. Sensing a wider berth, her mother swayed, arms floating in the air and keeping rhythm with the wind.

The wind? A breeze blew by Adah cooling her flaming cheeks. She looked up, past Ezra, higher than the gate. A droplet splattered on her nose. Rain!

Adah gripped her mother's hand. "Grab the other," she said to Judith.

Exaggerating the motion of her mother's sway, Adah hopped side to side. Humming a psalm, she danced.

Water fell from the sky and hit the dry ground. Drops vanished in tiny puffs of smoke.

Another lick of rain touched Adah's cheek. "God hears our praise. He sent the rain." She flapped her arm as if to fly to her God.

"It is not enough for a weed," a man uttered. "We will need more than this sprinkle."

Leah stepped forward and latched onto Adah's free hand. Beulah followed her daughter's lead. Their neighbor's belly took prominence in the center of the circle of women.

Wait one more day for a birth, Lord.

The disgruntled man scowled at their folly. Adah flashed him a bared-teeth smile.

"Rejoice," she sang. "We do not need a flood. God will hear our prayers tomorrow."

And she would pray tomorrow, tonight, and forever, for a soaking rain and the return of Othniel and Telem.

Though at this moment, she would praise the Lord, with her mother and sister at her side. For seeing Judith delighting in God's blessed rain was a lavender balm on Adah's battered heart.

34

Adah balanced a jug of olive oil on her shoulder and hurried to her storeroom. Three Sabbaths had passed since the king's procession had entered Jerusalem. She had filled the crafted jars with her original perfume and had sent them to the palace with the official messenger. She had mixed the additional scent Zipporah recommended for the queen's noblewomen. A hint of vanilla added to violet buds and moss made the new fragrance almost as intoxicating as her initial gift. One more batch and her work would be done. Another envoy would be on their way to the royal residence.

Rephaiah and his overbearing son Gershom sauntered toward her on the opposite side of the street. She shifted the oil jug to her other shoulder and averted her eyes, feigning interest in a basket weaver seated outside an alley. A few more steps and she would be two dwellings away from her sanctuary.

"Daughter of Shallum?" An urgency rushed Rephaiah's summons.

Her muscles knotted. She did not have time for a confrontation. If only she could scramble out of the ruler's sight, but his loud voice had passersby glancing her direction. Even the weaver halted her craft. She turned slowly, digging deep into her belly to force an almost-smile, an act of respect to make her mother and father proud.

"Ruler." She ignored his son. "This oil is heavy." True. "And I am in a hurry to finish a fragrance." Another truth.

"Of course." He scurried closer. "That is what I have need of?"

"Sir?" She shifted the jug again so Rephaiah could not pluck it from her shoulder.

"My wife is frantic for one of your perfumes. There is talk all over the city of your skill." He untied a pouch from his braided belt. "What do I owe you for a small jar?"

She stared at the gold coins pinched between his fingers. Her mouth soured. Straightening, she stepped backward as if the coins were diseased. Heat flushed her cheeks. This was the man who showed no mercy to Othniel's family? Did he believe the hardship he caused was forgiven?

"Well?" Rephaiah rubbed the coins together.

The *scritch* of his money did not entice her. "I don't know."

"You must," Gershom said. "My father is making a generous offer."

Adah pressed her lips together lest she give a harsh rebuke. Rephaiah and Gershom were responsible for withholding the news of the governor's arrival from her father. They meant to shame him and her family. Surely still, Gershom coveted her father's position.

Adonai give me wisdom.

Balancing the jug on her shoulder, she rubbed the gemstone Nehemiah had given her. Didn't it belong to King Solomon, David's son? The wisest king of all.

Her bones felt as light as the morning trade winds. What Rephaiah meant for evil, God meant for good.

She would not have offered a new perfume to the queen had her father had time to purchase embroidered garments or artisan jewelry for Nehemiah.

Toda raba, Adonai. Her heart softened. She blinked, smiling as smooth and regal as a fresh-bloomed lily. "I truly do not know the answer to your question. Zipporah handles the sale of my perfumes." And the price may double. "I believe she is in the marketplace as we speak. You are well acquainted, I believe."

"Of course," Rephaiah grumbled.

"Come, Father." Gershom strutted a few steps. "I told you she wouldn't know about trade."

I've just become wiser. "Shalom." Adah stifled a giggle as she continued on her way.

Bumping the door to her storeroom open with her hip, she placed the jug on her work table and halted mid-step. Perched in her war-battered window was a lizard. "Go away," she yelled. She couldn't risk a skink traipsing over her shelves making her leaves and buds unclean. She tossed a small root at the wall.

Was it dead? She inched closer and readied another root to fling. "Go away."

The lizard remained motionless. It wasn't alive. It was worn wood with nubbed feet and dirt eyes. Her skin tingled.

"Go away?" the deep, familiar voice echoed. "I just arrived."

Adah stifled a scream and whipped around.

There he stood in the corner. Her friend. Her love. Her Othniel. Knees weak and spirit soaring, she practically flew into his arms.

35

Othniel wrapped her in an embrace, not too tight, but with enough pressure that she could feel the boom of his heart.

She nestled her face into his dark curls. His skin was warm and he smelled of sunny days and afternoon breezes. To leave his arms would be torture, but with an open window and a door ajar, she eased enough to separate their bodies. For now.

She stroked his beard. He was truly here, in her storeroom, and not in a dream. "I prayed God would watch over you and bring you back to Jerusalem." Tears welled in her eyes. "Truthfully, I prayed He would bring you back to me." She blinked back the wetness threatening to spill. "I've missed you so much."

"You were always with me." He slid his hand down her side and rested it upon her hip, holding her close. "Every time I unearthed a root or found a new flower, I hid it away for when I returned." He drew her wrist to his face and inhaled against her skin. "Mmm, violets. You're my blossom." His voice was but a soft rumble. "I had to come back."

His breath rushed by her cheek and caressed every bone in her body.

Reaching for his hand, she lifted it from her waist to her lips, and kissed it. "God did not forsake us."

"No, He did not." His smile lit up the corner like a

freshly oiled lamp. "And I hear your perfumes are sought by all of Persia."

"Did you hear that on the street, or did you call on your mother?" A hint of disappointment choked her words. She wanted to be the first woman he sought.

"I saw her briefly." He swept a finger across her lower lip.

How could she complain about his visit home when his gaze beheld her like an angelic vision and her lips begged for another touch?

"My mother is busy bartering again because of you." He let go of her hands and stepped backward into the shadows.

No!

But then he took both of her hands and drew her close once again.

Yes!

Othniel leaned in, his expression serious. "Telem came and arranged for my release."

"Telem?" An excited shiver chilled her flesh. Could her joy be more complete? "Did he return with you? Is he in the city?"

"He's here, and I believe he's seeking your father." He raised his eyebrows as if what he was going to reveal was well known between them. "About Judith."

She squeezed Othniel's hands. "Oh, to see Judith so happy. How did he find you?"

"I don't know." Othniel caressed her skin with his calloused fingers.

The pattern he branded into her hand with his firm hold and wandering thumb caused her mind to lose all thought.

"Telem helped me prepare my master's fields so I could leave. He paid the price for my freedom."

Master? She stiffened. *Thank you, Lord, for freeing my Othniel.* "I will have to thank Telem for returning you to me."

"Then it will be mutual." Othniel sobered. "For I believe he is grateful we sought him to leave his cave and return to the city." A teasing grin burst forth. "Never once in Kadesh-Barnea did he ever call me 'boy.'"

She rocked forward in awe of how God was working in her life. God had not forsaken His servants. "I believe Telem is in love with my sister."

"I know about love." Othniel slipped a finger underneath her necklace. Every rotation of a bead sent a flutter through her chest.

"From what I saw and heard on the path home, Telem intends to be your brother-in-law." He stilled his hand. "As for me..." His breath, soft as a petal, bathed her chin. "I intend to be your husband. If you'll have me."

Selah! "Yes," she blurted out with a slight hop that pinned him in the corner. His declaration almost buckled her knees, but she held fast, for there was no other place she wanted to be than here with her Othniel. "I would be honored to be your wife."

He steadied himself. "I don't have much to offer you. I'm the fifth son of a man with parched lands."

"I've known that fifth son all of my life. He led me through the darkest cave." She matched his stunning smile, but even in all her happiness, thoughts raced through her mind of time and place and orders. She bit her lip.

"What is that frown?" His grip tightened as if he expected her to slip away.

"I have several orders to fill—"

"And I know where to find everything you need." With a glance toward the door, he pulled her closer. "Make all the fragrances you want. When we wed, your buyers will have to wait."

Her stomach jumped and twirled at the image of a marriage bed. "For how long?"

"Until we are ready." And like the day he arrived at Zipporah's storeroom and found her the pearl bottle, he bent forward and bestowed upon her something she needed. Needed desperately. A long and tender kiss. The kind of kiss she had desired while he was away.

When she caught her breath, she paid him back in abundance.

36

Adah rushed past the temple courtyard. Beads of perspiration formed on her brow as the afternoon sun baked her head covering. More orders needed filling.

She kept her betrothed busy bartering in the marketplace with the help of his mother. Praise be, Othniel agreed to live under her father's roof once they were married. Her storeroom was only a saunter from the front door, a convenience if she was late getting out of bed. *My Othniel.* A blush warmed her cheeks. No one would notice with the sun so high.

Telem had purchased a dwelling not far from her home. No one knew where he got the coins. What do you find in a cave to trade? It didn't matter as long as Judith was happy and lived nearby.

"Woman," a deep voice called.

Adah turned. She would know that summons anywhere.

"*Shalom,* Governor."

Nehemiah strode closer in an alabaster and indigo robe free of dust and sweat. His expression was as smooth as a newly budded leaf. He held a scroll aloft like a king holds a scepter.

"I'm glad I saw you." He nodded. "*Shalom.*".

She bobbed her head in a show of respect. "I am fleeing the crowd in the marketplace."

"I hear a request came from Egypt."

"It's true. Several orders were delivered by messenger." She smiled boldly. "Ever since Telem has been assisting my father, nothing stays quiet."

"What a blessing it is to finally be informed." He winked and then bent forward and began unrolling the scroll. "I thought you might like to read this before it is presented to the officials. I had to pry it out of a scribe's hand." Holding open a page, he grinned as if the squabble with the priest was notable.

Squinting at the perfect script, she read locations around Jerusalem and familiar names. Half-way down the page, she saw it. She saw her father's name listed among the names of other men.

"Shallum son of Hallohesh," she read aloud. "Ruler of a half-district of Jerusalem." Pressure built behind her eyes. She would not cry. Woe to any tear that spilled on this most important scroll. "Repaired." Her voice faltered, but her chest nearly burst open with pride. "With the help of his daughters."

Adah stepped back and swiped a tear from her cheek. Her vow was complete, and her father's name was recorded for all to see. Now and forevermore.

"You know what I regret?" Nehemiah carefully rolled the scroll. "That the priests did not record what I remember most." He paused and swallowed hard. "That a young girl standing on these rocks challenged grown men to be strong and courageous for their God."

Her spirit took flight. She tried to smile but her lips just quivered. "You forget where I would be without a cupbearer to the king who taught me that my strength and joy come from God."

Nehemiah's eyes glistened. He kissed the parchment listing the laborers. "It would seem,

Daughter of Shallum, that when God spoke to our hearts, we both listened."

"And heard," Adah whispered. "*Selah.*"

Thank you…

for purchasing this Harbourlight title. For other inspirational stories, please visit our on-line bookstore at www.pelicanbookgroup.com.

For questions or more information, contact us at customer@pelicanbookgroup.com.

Harbourlight Books
The Beacon in Christian Fiction™
an imprint of Pelican Book Group
www.pelicanbookgroup.com

Connect with Us
www.facebook.com/Pelicanbookgroup
www.twitter.com/pelicanbookgrp

To receive news and specials, subscribe to our bulletin
http://pelink.us/bulletin

May God's glory shine through
this inspirational work of fiction.

AMDG

You Can Help!

At Pelican Book Group it is our mission to entertain readers with fiction that uplifts the Gospel. It is our privilege to spend time with you awhile as you read our stories.

We believe you can help us to bring Christ into the lives of people across the globe. And you don't have to open your wallet or even leave your house!

Here are 3 simple things you can do to help us bring illuminating fiction™ to people everywhere.

1) If you enjoyed this book, write a positive review. Post it at online retailers and websites where readers gather. And share your review with us at reviews@pelicanbookgroup.com (this does give us permission to reprint your review in whole or in part.)

2) If you enjoyed this book, recommend it to a friend in person, at a book club or on social media.

3) If you have suggestions on how we can improve or expand our selection, let us know. We value your opinion. Use the contact form on our web site or e-mail us at customer@pelicanbookgroup.com

God Can Help!

Are you in need? The Almighty can do great things for you. Holy is His Name! He has mercy in every generation. He can lift up the lowly and accomplish all things. Reach out today.

Do not fear: I am with you; do not be anxious: I am your God. I will strengthen you, I will help you, I will uphold you with my victorious right hand.

~Isaiah 41:10 (NAB)

We pray daily, and we especially pray for everyone connected to Pelican Book Group—that includes you! If you have a specific need, we welcome the opportunity to pray for you. Share your needs or praise reports at http://pelink.us/pray4us

Free Book Offer

We're looking for booklovers like you to partner with us! Join our team of influencers today and periodically receive free eBooks!

For more information
Visit http://pelicanbookgroup.com/booklovers